Also by Ellis Sharp

I0542582

**Novels**

*The Dump*
*Unbelievable Things*
*Walthamstow Central*
*Intolerable Tongues*
*To Wetumpka*
*Lamees Najim*
*The Orwell Girl*

**Short Fiction**

*The Aleppo Button*
*Lenin's Trousers*
(with Mac Daly) *Engels on Video*
*To Wanstonia*
*Driving My Baby Back Home*
*Aria Fritta*
*Quin Again and other stories*
*Dead Iraqis: Selected Short Stories*

**Non-Fiction**

*Sharply Critical*

# NEGLECTED WRITER

## Ellis Sharp

**Zoilus Press**

A Zoilus Press paperback
First published in Great Britain by Zoilus Press in 2021

© Ellis Sharp 2021

A CIP catalogue record for this book is available from the
British Library.

ISBN 9781999735999

Cover design by The Ever-Shifting Subject

Typeset by Electrograd


ZOILUS PRESS
York, England

*Inspired by actual events*

# 1

THE PHONE AT THE BEDSIDE tore his dream wide open. He didn't remember much about the dream. He was in a strange house and he had to get out fast by the back door. But when he got to it the door was hidden behind a panel. He swung the panel open and behind it was a smaller panel. Behind that, a smaller one. Panel after panel. They ended in a hole that was big enough for a cat but too small for someone like him.

He liked the story. It had potential. Maybe he could have used it if he'd known what was coming next. But he never got the chance. That damned phone. The legendary caller from Porlock, Texas.

The twin ringing pulses of the phone traversed the room like carefully organised bursts of machine gun fire. *Traversed*. A damned fine word, he thought. His head hurt. When he shut his eyes there were horizontal lines of throbbing red. When he opened them the lines stayed there for several seconds before they melted. *Traversed*. It was the sort of word they don't let you use in Hollywoodland. Out here they'd insist on *crossed*. Keep it monosyllabic, Bub, they'd say. Don't bamboozle the audience. Make it clean and keep it short, amigo. And most of all: pack it with a punch.

The first Monday in September 1932. It would be another hot day. He took up the black mouth. What time was it? Too early. The room had a milky light. The curtains looked like dawn was hiding behind them but wasn't ready to come out yet. Dawn was a shy girl at first. Later she wouldn't be. Just like... he couldn't remember her name.

'Yeah,' he said.

'Eliot Blunt?'

'Yeah,' he said. Hot wet wiry stuff inside him tightened when he heard his name spoken like that. People who said his name like that were usually bill collectors or cops. But the tension eased, just a little, when he realised it was a woman on the line.

She was doing a lot of heavy breathing but Eliot didn't flatter himself she was pulling any funny tricks on his account.

The atoms of Eliot's attention dispersed, swarmed round the interruption, and let percolate those two magical words.

'Shoot,' he said. He'd come out from England seven years back but by now he'd learnt the language of the natives. A strange, slurred, hopped-up lingo, greased with fractured infinitives and double negatives.

There were more snuffles and loud breaths and then she spat it out.

*'Burns is dead!'*

This was accurate, he thought. The poet had been dead a hell of a long time, too. Two centuries maybe. Maybe a little more. As Eliot absorbed the woman's words, she added: 'I wanted you to know.' More snuffles. 'I've heard you're a guy who likes literature. You *know* stuff. You get the big picture. You've read a heap of novels. You can judge what's good and what's bad.'

This was indubitably true. Eliot Blunt had one of the finest sensibilities in California. It often felt strange that he had so few admirers. His rejected screenplays were piled in a box under the bed. His two novels had been turned down by agents and publishers from Des Moines to Detroit, from Delaware to Dallas, from Tacoma to Tuscaloosa. Only his journalism and his essays had sold. But word of his analytical intelligence had evidently gotten around. He was charmed by this woman, whoever she might be. He had never been much interested in the productions of the Ploughman Poet but he decided to do his best for her. He practically screamed the lines: 'Wee, sleekit, cow'rin, tim'rous beastie, O what a panic's in thy breastie!'

There was a long silence. He thought she'd gone. But the line didn't have the dead sound of a broken connection. Then he heard her breathing again. Finally she said: 'Are you drunk? Why are you talking in French? I'm not kidding. *Burn is dead!'*

Thunder crashed in the hills. Lightning flickered. The dancing atoms of his attention adapted themselves to a new scenario. Where there had once been a blur there was now perfect focus. Even Eliot's hangover seemed mellower. The horizontal lines had become a charming buttercup yellow. 'Did you say Burn? I'm terribly sorry. I thought you said Burns. As in Burns the poet.'

'Poet? I don't know no poets. You *are* drunk, aren't you, Mr Blunt?'

'If I am intoxicated it is only by life's many wonders and the manifold and unexplored possibilities of the novel form.'

Now she was crying. Eliot knew he had that effect on women. They never understood his sense of irony.

'Who is Burn?' he asked. He didn't know anybody called Burn.

Just then the warm soft body beside him in the bed stirred and muttered something.

The whimpering down the line once more transformed itself into language. American language. The words dragged out, rich with strange depths and echoes. 'Say – is there someone with you?'

He looked at the contours formed by the sheets. He was

reminded of the South Downs back in England. A chalk landscape full of delicious curves and grassy valleys.

'Nobody,' Eliot said. It was a gag from one of his many rejected screenplays. It featured a joker called Nora Nobody.

'I'm talking about Paul,' the woman breathed. Her voice was familiar but he couldn't place it.

Eliot was tempted to quip: 'That guy is a saint!' but he repressed the urge. Then his cerebral cortex connected the gist of the information which glittered in the dark and muddy depths of his confusion. The swirls of grit settled around a diamond as big as the Ritz.

The caller's voice trembled. 'He shot himself in the head!'

'You mean Paul Bern? *The* Paul Bern?'

'I just wish I'd never written what I wrote!' the woman wailed.

Then she cut the connection.

Maybe she was nuts, Eliot thought. How could Paul Bern be dead? He was in his prime. Eliot had seen him on the studio lot only the other day.

The other woman involved in this opening scene, the woman under the sheet beside Eliot, hauled herself up against the headboard. 'Was that your wife?'

'I've had two wives,' he said. If it had been a script he'd have written: *Eliot shrugs*. Or maybe: *Eliot briefly touches his heart then shakes his head and gives a wry smile*.

But life isn't a screenplay, movies are for sentimentalists and losers, and novels secrete spurious meanings to keep you consoled in the cold and the dark. You want life to be *War and Peace* but it ends up being *The Life and Opinions of Tristram Shandy*.

'It wasn't either of them.'

'You sure there isn't a third?'

'After the second wife there is no other,' Eliot said.

'Never say never,' the woman replied.

He remembered her name, now. Mildred. In the short time they'd known each other she'd claimed to be 37. That meant she was probably 43. Maybe even 47. You could never tell with women who occupied this particular spectrum of flesh and age.

*Of Flesh and Age* – what a title! Eat your heart out, Somerset Maugham. Now all he had to do was write the novel.

Two nights ago Mildred had stared into the depths of the tall glass where gin blurred by bitters kept a bunch of ice-cubes afloat. There was fruit in there, too. A tangerine curl. A half-moon slice of apple. A cherry or two. Any moment, Eliot thought, and I'll start seeing tiny goldfish. He enjoyed this brief flashback to their first evening. Since then he'd seen quite a few animate figures flickering in the dark depths of their short companionship and along the bright margins. Ants. Millipedes. A slow, golden cockroach.

He hadn't mentioned them. It's best not to tell a new lover about your demons. Women rarely understand, unless they suffer them too.

As Mildred downed the second glass that night she'd told him with a high proud glassy sharp enduring laugh how she'd burned through three husbands. She'd wanted to be an actress but had settled for secretary. Mildred knew what she wanted. She wanted to be rich. The next best thing to fame is a rich husband. She was still dreaming of hooking a producer, maybe, or an actor on the way down who might miraculously reverse his career trajectory. There was no future with a screenwriter but she needed other things in life than fancy clothes and a better car. She figured he might do for a night or two.

Their lives had collided in a joint off Wilshire Boulevard. It was the start of the Labor Day weekend. It was dark in there. He was sat on a stool reading a novel by the light of two whiskeys. Mildred came out of nowhere and slid on to the stool beside him. She glanced at the book. 'Mrs Dalloway,' she said. 'I don't know her books. Any good is she?'

'Not as good as Jacob Zroom,' he replied.

'Crime, yes?' She giggled. 'It's all anyone reads these days.'

Eliot knew that when a strange woman drops in on to the bar stool next to you it's for one of two reasons. She's either selling or she's giving. If she's giving there's a price too but it's usually cheaper. Eliot had the whole night ahead of him and some more after that. He was happy to slide there on a sled of conversation and alcohol.

They exchanged radically abbreviated finely polished autobiographies. He told her about the novel. It was the first in a crime series. Dalloway had invented a private dick whose only name was Woolf. A tough guy with a vulpine look about him. He operated out of Richmond. Hence the nickname.

Eliot reckoned he must have lived up to expectations because she was still with him after two nights. The next thing she drawled was: 'Give it to me again, big boy.' Her hand slid down across his body. He pushed her fingers away. He let the thumb remain. She sure knew her way around bedroom matters.

Hell, that was a good title. *Bedroom Matters*. Or was it too close to the edge? Too risqué, perhaps. As for Mildred. As a second-hand book she'd have been worth a punt. He could see the sales notice. *In reasonable condition. Some light soiling but internally tight and clean.*

'Later, sweetheart. I need to visit a corpse. I have to be sure he's what the lady says he is. Inert and likely to remain so.'

'So who was that whore on the phone?'

'She never gave her name. And I never had time to ask.'

'Who's the stiff?'

'If it's true what she told me, then it will be all over tomorrow's front pages. But it might just be some ex of mine with a twisted sense of humour. Or it might be a trap.'

'A trap!' Her eyes widened. It was a trick she'd learned from reading pulp novels and drama lessons. She narrowed them. 'You'd better pack some heat.'

'Baby, that's not my style. I'm English, remember? Why, I don't even know how to load a gun, let alone shoot it. Besides, I have no enemies and no debts.'

That last part wasn't strictly true. No matter. He kissed Mildred fiercely on the lips and then gently on her aureoles. 'I'll be back,' he winked.

'You'd better be, lover.' Her face was merry, with a hint of hunger and greed. But her mind was hidden. The reader would have to wait to see if she would ever be allowed inside it.

Eliot dressed hurriedly and breathed slowly. He paused to look at himself in the full length mirror on the wall. Not bad, he thought. But then, after all, he was young as the century. Plus California had been good for his complexion. Instead of English pink it was now dark as fine-roasted coffee. Heck, he was in his prime. He'd been born in Coxwold on the first day of the cruellest month, in a year of double zeroes. Double zeroes always reminded him of shotguns and frightened eyes and firm warm breasts. A nurse he'd dated once told him he ought to see someone about what went on his mind and what came from his mouth and his pen. An alienist. But Eliot felt very strongly it was best to keep away from the witchdoctor fraternity. He distrusted their bow ties, their leather couches, their phoney dream-analysis. He'd read Freud's short story collection. He wasn't impressed. No one had dreams like that.

Example.

The dreamer stood before a little house with closed doors which stood back a little behind a pair of stately palaces. The dreamer's wife led him along the street and pushed the door open. The man then went into a courtyard which sloped slightly. Freeze-frame. Enter the bearded Austrian, holding in his fist an enormous Cuban cigar. He waves it about. He wants the world to know he's the man.

Anyone who has had any experience in translating dreams, he booms, can see this is all about *coitus a tergo.*

No, me neither sister.

Eliot had to go to the biggest library in L.A. to find a book which would translate that sneaky little lump of prissy obfuscation. And when he saw what it meant... he understood.

He knew this guy's type. A back-door man. Or would have liked to be. You could tell it was all in the smutty Austrian's bloated head. You could see this Freud guy was into porn. *It turned out that a girl had come to live in the dreamer's house who had attracted him and had given him the impression that she would raise no great objections to an approach of that kind.* Even in a pit of Babylon like the City of Angels no cutie ever gives out that kind of *impression.*

The sick Austrian pretended to be a doctor. But it turns out he invented a whole new branch of medicine from scratch. A snake-oil salesman who'd started up an industry. Jeez...

Eliot slipped a cigarette between his lips and lit it. It felt good. The cool firm tube in his mouth, the little crackle of fire rubbed into existence... He sucked and exhaled. The smoke ring rippled upward. It was like one of the rings of Saturn had been cut loose. Another terrific title floated across the vastness of his mind, then fell back into the blackness like a used-up shooting star. He exhaled another smoke ring. He blew Mildred a smoky farewell kiss.

She'd pulled off the sheet. She lay face down, her arms and legs stretched out to make an X.

'Do you have to go?' She raised her rump in an enticing manner. She exhibited a fine clump.

'It could be important. Wait for me, lover. Help yourself to whatever you can find. I'll be back in a jiffy.'

'A what?'

But he'd already left the room. A moment later and another chapter in his short life was almost over.

Jaunty orchestral music accompanied him to the roadster parked out front.

# 2

ELIOT WENT VIA MULHOLLAND DRIVE to Benedict Canyon. Hell, why not? There's one place everyone ends up at, no matter what route you take. A scenic diversion is always to be cherished.

Paul Bern lived just off Benedict Canyon Road, at 9820 Easton Drive. Eliot had only been to the property once before but he remembered the number. He had a strange gift that way. Total recall.

*Paul Bern.* It was hard to believe he was dead. Hell, it was only two months since the dude had married Jean Harlow. *Jean Harlow.*

But maybe it wasn't true. Maybe the phone call was some kind of twisted hoax. He'd soon find out...

The house and gardens of the Berns residence were built into one of the canyon's twisting, steep, wooded southern flanks. To get to the front door from Easton Drive you had to walk up a steep narrow path embedded in the slope. It was a stiff ascent that left you floppy at the top.

Eliot remembered all the steps he'd ever walked up in his life. The Monument in London, he recalled, had three-hundred and eleven. The arch that welcomed you to the Holkham estate had seventy-one. North of Broadstairs, at the end of the garden of a large house overlooking the Channel, there was a cliff and below it a small private pier on a remote unvisited beach. To get to that pier you had to descend forty creaking wooden steps. Or one less than that since the thirty-fifth had disintegrated.

An old girlfriend had once compared Eliot to an elephant, which he liked to believe was a tribute to his rare memory rather than his long nose. But with women you never really knew. It might have been an allusion to his belly, his penis or even his sturdy well-grounded legs. He just hoped she hadn't meant his ears.

Easton Drive was a nothing sort of dirt road that went off the highway in a rise so steep that seeing it Dr Freud would have popped any number of blood vessels. He'd have said the surrounding trees were hair and the road was aroused. You could guess where the tip of it was headed. Eliot shut the doctor from his mind. The guy was sick, no question.

There was already a car parked at the foot of Easton Drive, so Eliot slid in behind (don't tell the doc). He didn't want to risk his tires. Besides, he doubted his engine had the power to get him up an unmade road that steep. That had zero to do with his sexuality and everything to do with his understanding of the limitations of the internal combustion engine. It's not until you see smoke pouring from under the hood you learn even a Buick has its limitations.

Eliot parked. He walked. He went up the steep dirt road until he reached Paul Bern's gate. Number 9820. An elephant never forgets.

He started up the seventy-five steps, passing under wooden arches from which dangling copper lamps swayed in a gentle breeze. He could hear the splash of water from the artificial stream that cascaded across a series of boulders into a frothing pool below.

On the forty-first step he met Marx coming down the hillside towards him.

Sooner or later all writers met Marx, although some of them never knew it. He dressed like a bourgeois and was often a slightly remote figure at the studio. His track record of successes was extraordinary, although a lot of people weren't aware. Marx's writing credits included *His*

*Awakening*, *The Wanters*, *Forbidden Paradise*, *The Great Deception* and *Strange Cargo*. He did some film editing and post-production work on *Broken Chains* and *Hungry Hearts*. As a director he was behind *Wordly Goods* and *Tomorrow's Love*. As a producer he helped with *Torrent*, *The Getaway*, *Noisy Neighbors*, *Dynamite*, *The Rogue Song*, *Paid*, *Inspiration*, *Grand Hotel* and *Strange Interlude*.

Eliot had never met him person to person, though he knew him by sight. Nowadays Marx was a studio hotshot. He was currently the story editor. He basically ran the writing department. Marx had been very tight with Paul Bern. They went way back, it was said. New York days.

Marx was a Jew, which didn't bother Eliot. Culver City was full of them. Some were fat, some were lean and hungry-looking. Some had the eagle's profile; others didn't. Eliot wasn't prejudiced. For example. Where women were concerned he preferred meat to bone, but he didn't let it dictate his choices. He felt basically he was a regular guy.

With Jews... some you win, some you lose. They ran the show, everyone knew it. That's how it goes in Babylon. Heck, pretty soon the Gentiles would probably have to start wearing armbands. Fine by him. Sartorial matters meant nothing.

Okay, so Louis B. Mayer sure looked like a shark wearing glasses. But that observation meant no disrespect to sharks or spectacles.

Sam Marx held up his palms. 'You can't go up,' he said. His eyes tightened as he scrutinised the intruder. 'Who *are* you?'

'Eliot Blunt. I work at the studio.'

'Which department?'

'Yours. Writing. They called me in to do some work on *The Girl from Kansas*.'

'Yeah, right...' Sam Marx scowled. He looked distracted. 'Well like I said, buddy. You can't go up. The studio is handling this.'

'It's true then. Bern's dead.'

'Yeah, he's dead. The poor sap shot himself.' Marx pointed to the steps behind Eliot. 'That's the direction you need to go, Eliot.'

'Sure Mr Marx, sir. I'm on my way.'

The Jew followed Eliot down the steps.

Forty-one, forty, thirty-nine...

Back on the Canyon Road the hotshot was about to get into his car when he frowned and shouted, 'Say, buddy, how did you know?'

Eliot winked. 'A tip-off. I got a phone call. In this burg news travels fast.'

'I guess that's so.' Marx looked sad; upset. He climbed into his car and drove off. Eliot followed him down the road, turned right at the first junction, and parked there.

He stepped out of the car. It was quiet and still. Woodland smothered the side of the canyon, casting a giant shadow. He wasn't far from 9820. Eliot had been warned off the front entrance, so he'd try round the back.

Don't tell Dr Freud, he thought.

A bleak smile appeared on his warm face.


Eliot took out a pink-tipped match and struck it against his thumbnail. He lit the penultimate cigarette in his pack of Camels and headed up the side of the canyon. It was dense with trees. The shade was richly textured. His canvas shoes crunched on the brittle layer of fallen vegetation. Crisp leaves crackled and twigs snapped with a high sharp crack. Sweet fragrant tufts of onomatopoeia sprouted in the slope beside big grey embedded boulders. Something boomed faraway, like a muffled explosion, and reverberated softly around the canyon.

It took Eliot's eyes a minute or so to adjust to the transition from sun-slashed highway to the darkness. It was cooler here, too. He shivered.

Soon he was lost among the soaring, bunched trees. It was a place loaded with adjectives. He sensed that Turgenev was here, somewhere.

Eliot used some of the lower branches to haul himself up the slope. At times he leaned against one of the thicker trunks and regained his breath. There were moments of Joycean epiphany when he witnessed lonely bugs creeping across the bark on a mission. He admired their resolution and their sense of direction.

The woodland held a faint aroma of jasmine.

As he climbed he thought about *The Girl from Kansas*. It was a screwball comedy, packed with light comic deceptions. An ingénue arrives in Sin City and has to fend off the attentions of various men before she finds an Honest and True Love. Eliot had been given a few lines of the True Love's to polish. *I dream about you every night. I dream of the day when we can be together, just the two of us. We'll live in a house by the ocean and make babies.*

After fifteen minutes Eliot came to a narrow path which cut across the slope. It looked like it was made by animals, not people. Were there deer up here? Surely they'd all been shot. Americans liked killing animals, when they took a break from killing each other.

He turned off along the slender track, heading in the direction of the Bern residence.

*

The track came to an area of burned land, where the trunks of a few bare trees protruded from a waste of scorched earth. Eliot was reminded of a photograph he'd once seen of a Great War battlefield. Nothing but desolation and black trees stripped of every branch.

One of the annual California summer fires had burned here. But already a few green shoots were poking through the layer of dry ash and twisted blackened stumps. In the midst of death there is fresh life, he thought.

Heck, that thought made up a pretty good line of dialogue. Probably no use in a screwball comedy. But if the studio ever did a war movie... He could see Ronald Colman saying the line in a slow, dignified English manner. A moment worthy of Shakespeare. It would need thirty or so extras playing dead folk and the heroine – a smooth pink young thing, well equipped in the store frontage aspect – holding a sweet, chubby, grinning baby.

Babies were trouble, he knew. They never obeyed the director's instructions. They wouldn't smile when you wanted them to. They fell asleep, just like any studio lush. They broke wind and caused the expression on the lead actors' faces to change. Often they just burst into tears. They were worse than actresses.

But for a line like that you needed a baby. He was certain of it.

He trod gingerly on the peppery ash. It was soft as snow and grey as a politician's principles. From here he could see part of the distant Hollywood hills – but not that section with the big white thirteen-lettered sign. The sky was blue and clear and the early morning mist over L.A. had largely melted.

Not far away, hovering over a ravine, was a big black bird.

It seemed enormous. It made a brilliant opening shot in the movie of this day's tragedy. Paul Bern had shot himself. And now a huge sinister creature was floating over the valley of death. In fact it *was* Death. It was a symbol. Directors liked symbols – but you had to use them carefully and cunningly. Eliot grinned. Those thick vertical cacti you saw in desert scenes – they were not innocent succulents.

Hot damn! He suddenly realised what the bird was. It was the falcon – the famous one. It had been stolen from a private zoo in Malta and sold to a wealthy ornithologist who lived in Beverly Hills. The creature had escaped. There was a big reward for its capture. Five Franklins. But you had to catch it alive and uninjured.

Eliot regretted he had no breadcrumbs in his pocket. But life is like that, he reflected. When there's an unexpected falcon to be caught it's so easy to let the opportunity slip.

He walked on across the burned landscape.

The next time he looked the bird was gone.

He re-entered the woods (don't tell the doc). Another ten minutes took him to a ridge overlooking the canyon. And there it was, the Bern property, directly below. He recognised it immediately. There was no house like it, not even in a city that especially favoured the baroque, the bad, and the banal.

Paul Bern had gone for mock-Tudor meets Scottish-baronial with a touch of the witch's house in *Hansel and Gretel* and a turreted salute to mad Ludwig. A strange concoction which showed Paul Bern had been a dreamer. The house was far weirder than anything in the mental scenery of rich men asleep in Vienna. It had four levels, not three. It was pure Hollywood. No ranch house for Paul. He needed a reminder of Tudor England, where entertainment was serious business and they still produced The Big Man's timeless scripts. Bern had created fairyland to show every moist, hungry studio princess he was the frog they'd been looking for. And he needed a hint of European royalty to show how far he'd risen – risen! – from his humble old-world origins.

And now somewhere inside that fantasy house he was a cold, stiffening corpse.

It didn't make sense. The guy had everything. Even better than that he had *more* than everything. Married to Jean Harlow, for God's sake. *Jean Harlow!* The big blonde beauty. The thespian with thighs. The dynamite demoiselle with the damnedest derrière you ever did dream. The dearest, dishiest dame in Tinseltown.

There wasn't a man in town didn't think about some hot, dirty action with that cutie. But Bern had decoupled. He was defunct. He'd go no more a-roving.

But why would any man close the door on Jean Harlow?

What had gone wrong?

Eliot's brain raced.

Never mind your brain, you booby! This is no time for mind games. Think about Bern. *Why?* Why had the producer done this terrible thing? Was it a case of dyscalculia? Or was it dyscrasia? Did it involve dysgraphia? Dysentery? Dysmenorrhoea? Dyspepsia? Dysphagia? Dysphasia? Dysphonia? Dysphoria? Dysplasia? Dyspnoea? Dyspraxia? Dysthymia? Dysuria?

The question wouldn't go away. Why had Bern drilled himself?

Eliot took some deep slow breaths. There was the faint faraway odour of peroxide. Nothing in this neighbourhood seemed quite as it should be. But then every lungful of air taken in L.A. is air previously breathed by murderers, adulterers, cops and dope fiends. A little dizzied by thin, tainted oxygen, Eliot gazed down at the steeply sloping garden. It was fragmented by ledges of rock and stone walls and zig-zagging paths. Trellis-framed patios revealed glimpses of quaint curly wooden furniture shipped from a Bavarian hunting lodge. Open sooty fireplaces stood beside neat stacks of logs. There were grottoes where small-breasted blank-eyed temptresses flaunted their plump curvaceous stone bottoms.

Even the paving of the paths around the house was crazy. The pool though was average. The water looked dark green and queasy. It was reflecting the trees. The pool had probably witnessed something of what had happened. But water can't speak about anything except itself.

Eliot could see a bunch of people down there, standing beside the pool. Half a dozen men, talking animatedly. He was too far away to hear what they were saying.

On the other side of the pool a colored man was sweeping leaves. That would be the gardener. There were always small, essential roles for genial and respectful black folk.

Eliot began to descend. He moved slowly from tree to tree. No one looked up; no one noticed him. By the time he reached pool level the gardener had left and the men had gone inside. A window was open and he could hear voices.

Eliot crept towards it. He'd almost reached it when a hard male voice behind him said: 'Hold it right there, buddy. Put your hands above your head. Do it real slow.'

Eliot performed the requested action.

'Now turn round.'

Ditto.

Facing him was a man with poor taste in shirts and a white

cowboy hat of the sort favoured by the natives of the Lone Star State. Eliot felt he was rehearsing a scene from one of the westerns that the studio bashed out at six weekly intervals. The plots didn't vary much. There was the good gunslinger, there was the woman from his past who was living in the little town where he showed up, there were the bad guys. The bullies were – bang! bang! – dealt with. Homely white racist settler order was restored. A misunderstanding was cleared up. Heck, it turned out that the Madame still loved the gunslinger! A happy ending.

Eliot looked at the man's gun. 'That's a .32, isn't it? It throws a lot of steel shavings. Better take care, my good fellow. You wouldn't want to get blood specks on that fine hat of yours.'

The man contorted his stubbly weather-beaten face, then spat. 'A limey, eh? There's too many like you in this town. Chauffeurs. Butlers. Phoney Lords. Sneaking pansies. You don't fool me. Take a look at the Bible, buddy. People like you are an abomination unto the Lord.'

The poor fellow had obviously never read Thomas Paine. 'I fear you misapprehend who and what I am,' Eliot said. 'Although in my younger days I was profoundly English I can assure you that I am not remotely homosexual in my erotic proclivities.'

'Just shut that big, soft mouth of yours, pal! What are you doing, sneaking around on private property?'

'Take me to your leader. I shall gladly explain.'

The man frowned. His brain whirled like a roulette wheel. Finally a thought – a decision – slotted into place. He indicated with the barrel of the gun: 'Step this way, Mac.'

They went inside, to where a group of men stood by the big medieval fireplace, talking in low voices. They turned and stared as Eliot and his companion entered.

'I caught this wise guy skulking around outside. Spying.'

Eliot felt the muzzle of the gun press against his spine. It was a not unpleasant sensation. He tingled and felt a little shiver spread down his back.

One of the men glared at him and said: 'So what's your game? Spill.'

Eliot would have liked to shrug but was fearful that a sudden movement of his shoulders might provoke gunfire or cause vibrations in the air which could very easily bring the crossed swords above the fireplace tumbling from their supports. That would result in a distressing clatter. So he remained absolutely motionless, apart from a slight opening of his lips.

'I got a phone call. So I thought I'd check it out. See if it was true that Bern was dead.'

'Phone call from who?'

'*Whom*,' Eliot said. The war against error never ends. Standards of grammar must be upheld otherwise chaos ensues.

His inquisitor scowled and appeared perplexed. But plainly the brute was uninterested in the niceties of language. 'Spill. Or get spilt,' the lout ejaculated.

'Heck, I don't know. The telephonic communicator of this sad tiding was, alas, anonymous.'

'Okay, Jack Horner. Go stand over there.'

Eliot went and stood by the head of a moose with big sad eyes.

Nearby in the house, someone flushed a lavatory. It was a homely, reassuring sound.

The men whispered.

'I say we get rid of him,' the man with poor taste in shirts advised.

More whispering. They seemed to arrive at a consensus; a decision.

The leader of the group called across the room: 'You must be thirsty. Tom here will get you a beer.'

'I say, that's awfully decent of you,' Eliot said.

Tom returned with a tall glass filled with a golden liquid, the beaded bubbles winking at the brim.

Eliot drank it down. It tasted of sweet, carbonated metal polish. He sighed, mentally. Americans were hopeless at the manufacture of beer. It was best to stick to their whiskey.

'So who sent you?'

'No one sent me.'

'In that case you're free to go.'

'I am? Well that's swell. Thanks a heap, guys. You've been awfully decent.'

Eliot made for the door but the sudden movement seemed to shake something in his head, as though his skull was a snow globe. But instead of small white flakes falling across the architecture of his mind all that clouded it was particles of mud. As the grit descended it seemed to do strange things to the rest of his body.

He took one slow dragging step, then another. He felt suddenly intoxicated. It was as though the barometer of his emotional nature was set for a spell of riot. Eliot closed his eyes. He tried to shake himself free of the bad weather in his head. He began to pant. He suddenly felt very, very cold.

His shoes wouldn't go where he wanted them to go. His legs felt like mush. A dazzling flash of lightning slithered inside the rusty machinery where he did his thinking. He finally understood what they'd done. Terror boiled up inside him. It hissed and popped. There was anger there, too. It rose in spires of fire.

'You dirty sons of bitches!' he shouted. But the sentence he'd produced seemed more like a whisper than a cry. 'I'll tear your guts out!' he croaked. His voice was hoarse and thin and small. 'You two-timing rats... you double-crossing...'

The dialogue would need some work but he felt his performance was remarkable. He was centre-stage. He swayed. He held out his arms, as if feeling his way forward in a darkened room. Next he became aware of dribble coming from the corner of his mouth. It was like being at the dentist's. But now he was numb all over, even down to his toes.

'Spiked my... burr,' he whispered, swaying. 'Can't... daw... thish... to... me...' He was about to topple.

'I warp fur... I work for... ' He managed to articulate the three magic letters before he fell.

'Em... gee... em.'

As he succumbed to gravity he had the briefest of glimpses of their faces registering recognition, shock and alarm. One of them – the leader – seemed to start forward.

Then Eliot hit the floor.

The shock was cushioned by a blast of pain that turned instantly into black night. It meant another chapter was over.

# 3

ELIOT WOKE ON THE BED of the Pacific Ocean. The water was crystal clear. Though it was deep where he was, sunlight still penetrated from above. A blue, warm world.

A nearby octopus gave him a friendly smile. Shoals of fish swam past, casting rushing shadows. The octopus walked over to a magic beanstalk and began clambering up it.

That was when Eliot saw the crab woman. She was lying face down in the sand, with her legs apart. She had big breasts and a substantial bottom. But her arms and legs ended in claws. A pair of long stalks protruded from her head. The tendrils of a slimy sea plant swayed between her thighs.

She had blonde hair and blue eyes. She didn't seem to notice Eliot. Somehow she reminded him of the sphinx.

Then Eliot saw Dr Freud. The Austrian moved into view like a miniature submarine. He had a boner big enough to harpoon Moby-Dick. Freud's strong, hairy arms chopped at the liquid world which kept him afloat. His propulsion was impressive and his beard and the hair on his head and around his groin were soft and dark and streamed like weed in a current.

He came silently at the crab woman, from the rear. His intent was plain.

She seemed entirely oblivious of the lecherous foreigner who cruised closer and closer. Sleekly, silently, he approached the oyster-like orifice. Or was it a walnut he was after?

Freud's face wore the smirk of a self-satisfied professor. He was emperor of this world and he sure as hell knew it.

The smooth mushroom head of his taut, tense tube was on the very brink of an entry when it happened.

The crab woman whipped over on to her back. Disturbed sand rushed upward like smoke.

As she turned, her claws snapped together.

Freud's penis was sliced off. *Chop!* Just like that.

It dropped gently to the ocean bed, making a slight to and fro movement like a falling autumn leaf. As it descended it trailed threads of dark blood. A moment later a shark entered the frame. It swooped at the tasty morsel and swallowed it in a single gulp. With a flick of its fin the predator was gone.

Freud's face was contorted with pain and shock. A huge red cloud billowed from his groin. It expanded until the whole screen was filled by a swirling scarlet fog. It forced its way past Eliot. He could taste blood and salt. His head hurt.

Then an alarm sounded, piercing the mist, dispersing the last particles of blood.

The ocean contracted and then evaporated as the twin ringing pulses of the phone filled the bedroom.

Eliot reached for the device.

'Yeah?'

'Don't say you weren't warned, buddy,' a harsh male voice rasped. 'You're finished.'

'Eh?'

'Don't bother coming in today. Not today or any day. You're fired.'

'Eh?'

'We don't employ lushes who can't keep time. And you, buster, sure as hell can't do that. You were warned – one more late morning and that was it. Well, you never showed up today and that's the end of it. Bye, pal!'

'But – but – my drink was spiked! I've only just woken up! What time is it?'

'Time you sobered up, pal. And don't try sneaking in. Your pass is void. The guys at the gate have been warned.'

'I – I – '

The line went dead.

Eliot groaned. He was in his bedroom on the fourth floor of the San Bernardino Arms, the curtains were closed, his head was hosting a party of road workers. They had drills and spades. They kept hitting electrical wires. When that happened there were flashes and bolts of pain. His head throbbed with burning sludge. When he closed his eyes he saw the grid again. When he opened his eyes he saw lines of scarlet poppies. The poppies hopped about a little.

He focused on the bedside clock. It was eleven in the morning. Mildred wasn't there. Hardly surprising. It was over twenty-four hours since he'd left her in this very bed.

Eliot went to the john. He tried to be sick but all he did was choke and gurgle. His throat burned. He emptied his bladder. The jet split into two, one greenish, one yellowish. Next he went to the kitchen. He felt incredibly thirsty. He drank two glasses of water, then made a black coffee, with four teaspoonfuls of sugar. He gulped it down and had another.

He was still dressed in the clothes he'd been wearing the day before. He peeled the garments off and went to take a shower. Afterwards he went back to bed and fell asleep.

When he woke it was 2pm. He felt better. His head had cleared itself of débris. He put on some clean clothes. Eliot felt hungry. He ate his favourite monosyllables – ham and eggs. He didn't let the call from the studio upset him. He was more worried about the number of sentences in his life beginning with 'He'. His creator had been reading too much pulp fiction. Eliot sighed. It was good to sigh. He knew for a fact from Charlie Leadbeater it was good for your chakras.

No matter. However lamentable the style of his current predicament might be he'd find a way back in. There were people he knew. Someone would put in a good word for him. There were so many to choose from. Cerebral. Conceptive. Suppositional. Percipient. Experimental. Bibliophiliac. Attentive. Contemplative. Considerate. Diligent. Vigilant. Enthralled. Obsessive. Monomaniacal. Pedantic. Meticulous. Fastidious. Neurasthenic. Brilliant. Alcoholic. Fixated. Fetishistic. Maladjusted. Slovenly. Elated. Besotted. Scatterbrained. Eccentric. Whimsical. Ironic.

He looked for the note from Mildred. She must have left him one, somewhere.

But she hadn't. He looked everywhere. Ah, well. She had his number. It was 69. She knew where he lived. He felt sure she'd be back. Then he realised everything wasn't as it had been when he'd departed. Things had been disturbed. Someone had been through his drawers, his cupboards, his wardrobe. His books on the shelf weren't in the right order! *Red Harvest* and *The Glass Key* had flanked a pioneering work of literary analysis which concluded with the observation that *The concluding pages, a passage of vivid lyrical beauty (which I quote* in extenso*), are at once intensely personal and symbolic of the divine love of Nature for her children, a springsong of the Earth.* But now they were parked together to the left of that volume.

Worse, several of his Woolfs were missing! That could only be Mildred. She'd cleaned him out. She'd left the also-rans and taken the good stuff – *Jacob's Room, Mrs Dalloway, To the Lighthouse.* Worst of all, she'd made off with *The Waves.* He could replace the others but he could never substitute for that last title, because it was a signed first edition. *To Eliot from Ginny, hugs and kisses my sweetest platypus* xxxxxxxxx.

The phone rang. That would be Mildred. He had so much to tell her. Plus he wanted *The Waves* back.

But the woman who spoke wasn't Mildred. And it wasn't the cutie who'd tipped him off about Bern's death either. This woman spoke in a purr – a soft, velvet-lined voice. You could practically smell the perfume.

'Is that Eliot Blunt?'

'Uh huh.'

'Mr Thalberg would like to talk to you. We're sending a car.'

'I don't know any Thalbergs.'

'Is that Eliot Blunt who works for M-G-M?'

'It is.' He said it before he remembered that the present tense was no longer applicable.

'I'm speaking of Irving Thalberg, Mr Blunt.' There was a silky pause. There was what sounded like whispering and female giggles. She continued. 'He's a producer at M-G-M. He really would like to see you very much. It's urgent.'

Eliot thunk. He wondered what kind of underwear this woman wore. Probably black, lacy, exciting. He jolted his mind back to the primary topic. 'I'd be happy to speak to Mr Thalberg,' he said. Hell, yes! Thalberg – *that* Thalberg – was the second top man at the studio.

'The car will be at your door shortly.'

'Thanks awfully. Incidentally, sister, would you mind telling me – '

But the woman had put the phone down.

Eliot was attending to his hair when the doorbell rang. He ran downstairs.

The studio driver was a cross between an English bus conductor and an aviator. A cap, a uniform, gloves and goggles. Amusingly, the fellow was English. He said his name was Reginald.

'Been here long, Reg?'

'Quite some time, sir, yes.'

'Ever go back to Blighty?'

'No. Why would one choose to go back when one was in California, sir?'

'Quite. Family?'

'Mother deceased, father diseased. Sisters married to drunken coal miners. No longer in touch.'

'Ah.'

Reg added in a furtive whisper: 'They live under a terrible shadow. They firmly believe D.H. Lawrence is an important novelist and thinker.' For a moment his voice cracked and his face was one of anguish. 'I had to get away from all that.'

'You poor fellow. I quite understand.'

The high white walls of the studio came into view. At the auto gate entrance there was the usual crowd. Sixty or so fans, hoping to glimpse a star. Most of them were women. As the driver slowed, one of them jumped on to the running board. A big, beefy woman. She fixed her fierce attention on Eliot.

'Nah!' she screamed. 'He's nobody!'

The fans fell back, stricken with disappointment. Eliot's driver rolled slowly through their indifference, to the tall round pillars. In the shadow of the portico arch the guards didn't ask for passes. They recognised the car and the driver and waved the vehicle past. A minute later the driver was beside Eliot, holding the door open. 'In there, sir.'

Eliot knew the building. Three storeys with long balconies and iron rails, in a corner on Washington Bouelvard. It was where the big shots hung out, including Louis B. Mayer. Eliot had never been inside. He walked up the steps and into the lobby. A black man wearing a braided red uniform loitered in the space close to a desk where a brunette receptionist with small taut breasts watched him approach.

'I'm Eliot Blunt. Mr Thalberg is expecting me.'

She manufactured a brisk insincere smile and talked into a phone. She talked, she listened, she said: 'Sure'. And then: 'If you wouldn't mind waiting over there, sir.'

She indicated some armchairs on the other side of the lobby. The upholstery matched the fabric worn by the black man.

Eliot did not have to wait long. Almost at once a flunkey appeared, who escorted him to a small waiting room on the second floor. It was a bit part, not worth using any precious adjectives on. The bare minimum – an indefinite article, a noun, a verb. Get you gone, flunkey.

Up there, by the waiting room, three secretaries sat behind a large desk. One typed, the other spoke on a phone, the third was writing something down. The secretary on the phone was considerably younger than her colleagues. She was a redhead. Eliot heard her soft purring voice and guessed this was the one who'd phoned him about the chauffeur.

The waiting room had six chairs and a table bearing copies of *Photoplay*, *Motion Picture* and *Screenland*. There was also a door with a sign: IRVING THALBERG. Eliot had barely sat down when the door opened and Clark Gable stepped out. He looked worried. Then he saw Eliot and smiled. His smile expanded, his eyes began to twinkle.

'How goes it, feller!' Clark Gable patted Eliot on the shoulder, winked, and went on past the secretaries. 'My three beautiful babies!' he said. He blew them a kiss.

He seemed smaller than he did on a screen.

'Do come on in, Eliot,' Irving Thalberg said.

Eliot followed him into his office.

'Could you close the door, please.'

Eliot obeyed. He sat where he was invited to sit. The room was smaller than he'd been expecting. It was in a corner of the building, with windows allowing in dazzling Californian sunlight from two directions. But the incandescence was filtered and softened by shutters. Only a few bright lines had made it through to the floor. The pattern they made reminded Eliot of the throbs and lines of fire quietly bubbling inside his head.

Thalberg was his own age, Eliot saw. It was unbelievable that someone so young had risen so high, so quickly. He had a slim body, a soft face. He was wearing a dark jacket, buttoned up. A dark tie protruded from high stiff collars. He looked like he belonged in a bank or a funeral parlour, not a film studio.

Thalberg seemed worried. His face was almost grey.

'Thanks for coming in,' he said. 'The men told me what they did. I'm afraid that was out of order. I've told them something like this must never happen again. No ill effects, I hope?'

'I don't feel too good actually. My head feels like a bucket of wet sand.'

'I'm sorry. You must understand they had no idea you worked for us.'

'Us?'

Thalberg gestured. 'The studio. M-G-M.'

'I don't. I was fired this morning. For not turning up to work. Pretty funny, huh? Some guys from the studio make me late for work by spiking my drink, another guy from the studio fires me because at clocking-in time I happen to be unconscious. It would make a pretty fine comedy, wouldn't you say?'

'I didn't know you'd been fired. Don't worry about that. I'll fix it. You're in the writers' department, right? What's the picture you're working on?'

'A little number called *The Kid from Kansas*.'

'Oh that,' Thalberg said. There was disdain in his voice. *Disdain*. A certain lofty superior supercilious derisive scoffing scorn indicative of disrespect, irreverence, undervaluation, disparagement and ridicule.

'I doubt that script is going any place soon. But it's not why I wanted to see you.'

'And there's my car! Those jokers took me home, which I'm sure was mighty decent of them. But now my precious automobile is still back where I parked it yesterday. Just off Benedict Canyon Road and many miles from home. A fellow needs his wheels in L.A.'

'Don't worry about that Eliot. I'll get a studio driver to take you there when we're done. Now to get back to poor Paul Bern. What I'm curious about is this. *How did you know?* You were there before the cops.'

Eliot wasn't aware of that. But then again he hadn't thought about the strange absence of cops.

'I was tipped off. This dame rang me up. She didn't say who she was. She said Bern was dead. Of course I naturally assumed she was referring to the Scottish poet, Robert Burns. After we'd sorted out that little misunderstanding she said he'd shot himself and she wished she'd never written what she'd written. Then she put the phone down on me. I only went to Bern's home to see if it was true he was dead and to try and find out what this message meant.'

'And you have no idea who she was?'

'She wasn't anyone I knew, that's for sure. But her voice was vaguely familiar. Like a waitress who'd served me a meal, maybe. Or some dame in a shop. I sort of knew it – and didn't know it. It all happened so quickly. And I was asleep when she phoned. I was having this strange dream about a house, and there was this hatch, and underneath the hatch – '

'I'm not interested in your dream, Eliot. I'm interested in what this woman said about writing something she regretted.' Thalberg leaned forwards. 'This could be important, Eliot. Can you recall her exact words?'

'It was something like: *I wish I'd never written what I wrote.* Or pretty much that. But she never said *what* she'd written – what it was about. A love letter? A movie script? And why was she telling *me*? I wasn't close to Paul Bern. We weren't friends.'

'That's the mystery,' Thalberg agreed. He was silent for a minute, then another seven seconds after that he broke the silence. 'Let me level with you, Eliot. We have to protect Miss Harlow. We can't let this terrible tragedy drag her down. The fact is Paul Bern had physical problems. The poor man couldn't *do it*. He turned in a terrible performance. He felt humiliated. He felt he'd humiliated *her*. So he shot himself. He couldn't live with his impotence.'

'Goodness.' Who would have thought it? The guy was in bed with Harlow and he couldn't deliver. That was truly incredible. His nerves must have been shot to pieces.

'This tragedy plays hell with our schedules, Eliot. Miss Harlow is in the middle of shooting *Red Dust* with Gable. The poor kid is in a terrible state. We need to get her back working as soon as she's ready. In the meantime we have to wrap this matter up as quickly as possible. We don't want any scandal. That's why I'm relying on you, Eliot.'

'Me?'

'I want you to find out who this female was who phoned. Find out what she meant by writing something she regretted. Find out if she's on the level. We don't want any surprises. So far the studio has this thing under control. So we don't want crazy women popping up at the inquest with wild tales. We don't want anyone selling her story to the papers. So find this woman and report back.'

'I wouldn't really know how to go about that, Mr Thalberg. I'm not a private detective. I have no experience in these matters.'

'You said you thought you knew her voice. So all I'm asking you to do is to keep to your old routines. Hang out at the commissary and listen in. Go shopping at your regular stores. Visit your watering holes. Listen out for that woman's voice. And when you hear it... find out her name.'

'I suppose I could do that.'

'In the meantime, take it easy. Maybe she'll phone again. If she does, try and keep her on the line. Find out more about her. I'll arrange for you to have your own office in the writers' block. Just keep doing what you were doing before.'

'Back to *The Kid from Kansas*, then.'

'No, not that. Find something new. Maybe you could work on some original treatments. Are there any writers you know of we should be considering?'

'Virginia Woolf.'

'I've never heard of her.'

'She's done quite a few books.'

'Okay, Eliot. Pick out three or four of her books and write me one-page treatments. Short and snappy. But remember – make them adaptations. Change the plots if you need to.

Novelists often have no sense of pace. They spend too much time alone. They have no idea how real people act or the things they say.'

'Will do, Mr Thalberg.'

'My secretary will call a driver and you can go and collect your little automobile. Then go home. Drink lots of water. Get some rest. Come back to the studio tomorrow at nine. I'll have someone waiting for you with a new pass. They'll show you your office.'

Thalberg stood up and extended his hand. The interview was over.

Outside, the redhead was framed by two empty chairs. Eliot walked over and in a low direct voice asked her a question. She responded with a quick sharp merry slap on the face. His right cheek burned. He fell back and pressed his palm against the tingling skin.

'I expect you're the kind of guy who dreams of making a snowman,' she said. 'Only no matter how much snow you got it melts away before you've built him more than inch high.' She smirked. 'So beat it, buster. Head for the Alaska. Try your luck there.'

Eliot flushed. He knew what she was getting at.

'Freudist!' he spat.

# 4

ELIOT WAS IN AN EXCITED MOOD for the rest of the day. On the way to collect his car he asked the driver to stop at Schwab's. He darted out and bought cigarettes and some newspapers. He almost fainted in Schwab's. Everything started to fade. But the chapter couldn't be allowed to end in the first paragraph, so he pulled his selves together and tottered out. Language clung to him like flies on a rotting undiscovered corpse.

Later, reunited with his beloved roadster, Eliot drove to a small back-street establishment he knew well. He went along Los Angeles to Fifth, east to San Pedro, and then south via Zoilus Avenue to the neighbourhood where a shabby bearded Pole who went by the name of Korzienowski sold magazines, postcards and books, of the sort you didn't find in Main Street news vendors. The books were mostly imports, many from Paris. Eliot was in luck. Korzienowski had the four Woolfs that he needed the most. He handed over the outrageous sum demanded – *The Waves* was packaged as 'unmentionable perversion' and *Jacob's Room* as 'a tale of whips, leather and chains!' – and drove home.

Back at his apartment, he hurriedly sketched a treatment of *The Waves*. The movie should begin with a bank heist, he decided. It would be carried out by seven lowlifes. They were Woolf's characters – but given a little tweaking. Percival – that name would have to go. Make him Pierce 'Killer' Muldoon. Pierce is shot dead by a bank security guard but the other six escape with the loot. They hole up in a house by the ocean, waiting for the heat to die down. The waves lap remorselessly against the shore. The sound and rhythm is like that of a clock. It's the sound of Fate – of Destiny coming their way. As the hours pass the robbers' underlying antagonisms begin to surface. Make Neville a fat dubious East European. *Fatnev*. Fatnev is the driver of the getaway car. At the hideaway house he starts to crack up, getting on everyone's nerves. Flaky 'Reno' Rhoda, a nervy drug-taking depressive – she was Pierce's girl – attacks him with a knife. Ma Susan drags her off but is shot by 'Whispering' Louis, who says she and Fatnev have been planning to escape with the loot when everyone else is asleep. Ma Susan denies this but the dying Fatnev admits it's true. The gang leader, Bernie Harder, coshes Ma Susan and with Louis's help dumps her in the ocean. When they return to the house they find that Jinny, Harder's moll, has been locked in a side room and Rhoda has vanished with the loot. Later, Bernie returns with the dough, telling Jinny that Rhoda killed Louis, and he then shot her. 'There's just the two of us now, baby,' he says.

But neither of them know that Pierce didn't die but was seriously wounded. Angry that the gang left him behind, the dying man tells the cops where his associates have holed up. As dawn breaks the cops storm the house. Bernie runs for the pier where there's a speedboat moored but he's gunned down. Jinny is caught alive. As she looks down at Bernie's body being rocked to and fro in the surf Jinny sobs that she was forced into a life of crime and she has decided, once she has served her sentence, to become a nun. The jury find her Not Guilty and the film ends with Jinny praying for forgiveness in a convent beside the Pacific, while a beam of sunlight shines down on her and a choir of nuns sing an uplifting hymn. We hear the hymn as the camera tracks away across the convent grounds, ending with the waves slowly rolling towards the shore, while the sun sinks into the Pacific.

Eliot thought that was pretty good. Of course it was only a

rough draft but he felt it had potential. It gave Virginia Woolf's story added zest while basically staying faithful to her characters and all that stuff about time, relationships, etcetera. When you dipped into the novel it had some terrific dialogue. *Life is just a rushing stream of broken dreams.* And: *Once there was a wise-guy who wanted to write my biography – he died a long time ago.* And *Listen, everyone! Can you hear those dogs barking?* And *You're coming with me, sister – there's a richer, more complicated world out there and I'm taking you to it.*

Before he knew it he'd written three pages and the bottle of hooch was empty. Eliot set the treatment aside and turned to the newspapers.

BERN DEATH MYSTIFIES was the headline on the front of the *Los Angeles Times*. JEAN HARLOW'S MATE SUICIDE.

Bern had evidently shot himself in his bedroom. The body was found slumped in the closet doorway.

*Bern's suicide, according to police, apparently was accomplished after the manner of a death scene in* What Price Hollywood?, *a recent film release depicting the life of Hollywood film celebrities, in which the leading male character, tiring of what was termed 'an artificial life,' stood before a mirror and shot himself.*

Eliot had missed that movie.

He read on.

A detective had discovered a suicide note on top of a dresser.

> *Dearest Dear,*
> *Unfortunately this is the only way to*
> *make good the frightful wrong I have*
> *done you and to wipe out my abject*

*humiliation. I Love You.*
*Paul*

> *You understand that last night was only*
> *a comedy.*

Thalberg's words came back to Eliot. It all made sense. Bern felt an overwhelming sense of his inadequacy as a man. In marrying Jean Harlow he had humiliated her. He couldn't fulfil her needs or his own. He was a joke husband. There was no percentage in their marriage. There was only one way to end it...

By eleven Eliot felt exhausted. He was about to go to bed when the telephone rang. He decided to ignore it. It rang again ten minutes later. Again, he ignored it.

He went to bed and fell asleep at once.

Soon he was wandering in sunny dreamland, where he became reacquainted with Dr Freud. On this occasion Freud had taken on the form of a bearded elephant. The elephant was cautiously making its way along the top of the HOLLYWOODLAND sign. Behind the sign was an enormous clock, which showed that the time was ten to two. At the foot of the letter Y stood a young blonde woman with a large magnifying glass. She was looking for her husband.

Further along the hillside snow had fallen and a couple on skis were speeding downhill. Half way down the hillside some bodies were being burned. Expertly the skiers avoided the blackened, smoking area.

From a cloud in the sky a variety of numbers were falling. They were just a few inches in length and quite brittle. Sixes, nines, many zeroes. Several ones, which had been damaged and were bent over.

The elephant adopted a crouching posture and began to

squeeze a large tube of excrement from its rear. The excrement was a grey color and smelled of mint.

And then the telephone rang again.

This time Eliot answered it.

Wrong number. A man from Montgomery wanting a fellow named Richard Dover.

Eliot fell asleep again.

If there were other dreams that night he had no memory of them.

# 5

WHAT A WEEK that was!

On Monday there was the situation at a dead man's house.

On Tuesday there was Eliot's interview with Irving Thalberg.

On Wednesday the world learned that Paul Bern had a brother. His name was Henry. En route to Hollywood from New York his plane landed at Kansas City to refuel. Henry Bern talked to reporters at the airport. He threw them a name. *Dorothy Millette*. 'Paul was never married to her,' he said. He was quashing a rumour that didn't yet exist! No one had ever heard of this dame! What in hell was going on here?

*Nostrils flared.*

The press sniffed sweet juicy saleable scandal.

'Paul was never married before he wedded the screen star Jean Harlow, but he lived with a woman once, a long time ago,' Henry confided. 'He took care of her just the same as though she were his wife. He had been keeping her in a sanatorium. Miss Harlow knew of it because Paul told her. He concealed nothing but lived openly. Nothing was misrepresented when he married Miss Harlow, I know this.'

*The phantom wife!*

*Boys, we gotta find this broad!*

Problem was – nobody could...

That day Eliot went back to M-G-M.

He was given his new studio pass. He was shown to his writer's office. A secretary would be available when he needed one. In the meantime all he had to do was work on his Woolf treatments. *The Waves* was pretty much done. What next?

*Jacob's Room*, he decided.

A good title. Often the very finest novels had just two word titles. *Great Expectations. Wuthering Heights. The Miserables. Anna Karenina. To Wetumpka.* The same was true for movies. *Animal Crackers. Anna Christie. Back Pay. City Lights. Bad Girl.*

You only had to dip into *Jacob's Room* to see its potential. Rebecca catches a death's-head moth in the kitchen. Jacob is holding a different moth. The night he caught it a tree crashed down. That wasn't all. *There had been a volley of pistol-shots suddenly in the depths of the wood.*

The action would have to be shifted Stateside, obviously. The characters would need tweaking. And there was the title. Why was Jacob's room so important? It was more than just a bedroom.

Eliot lit a cigarette. He poured himself a tumbler of fake Old Forester.

This did the trick.

*Jacob's room was where the dope was kept.* But Jacob had gone – and so had the consignment! The gang went in pursuit – and so did the cops!

Eliot scribbled furiously, pausing only to shed ash and tears and to drink more whiskey.

He ate lunch at the commissary. He kept his ears open. But he didn't hear that voice.

Back in his office he fell asleep. Thinking sure was as fatiguing as writing.

Before Eliot knew it his day was over. He grabbed some food at a diner, then went home. He had an early night. The telephone never rang. He slept.

He went to a cinema to see *What Price Hollywood?* but inside there were just three people in the audience, all women. They were sitting in the front row together. The show hadn't started yet. As Eliot entered they stood up. A blonde, a brunette, a tall thin one with jet black hair. The blonde was twisting a small dead chicken in her hands. The brunette approached him with an overcoat. It was too small. The tall one said: 'Take mine.' She unbuttoned her white raincoat. Underneath it she was naked. She threw her raincoat onto the floor. Eliot stepped forwards, tripped and fell down.

The women started laughing.

Eliot said: 'I just want to hear you speak again.'

The tall one held a finger to her lips. She looked sad. She shook her head.

The women returned to their seats. The lights dimmed. The show began.

Where the dream went after that he'd no idea. Darkness intervened. It was like one of those novels which the writer never finishes because death arrives much earlier for her appointment than expected.

Next morning, the Thursday of that crowded week, Eliot drove to the Price-Daniel funeral parlor on Sawtelle Avenue. It was where the corpse was stored. It was where the inquest into the death of Paul Bern was to be held this very day. Eliot felt he ought to go. Maybe the woman on the phone would be there.

Hundreds of onlookers crowded the street outside the parlor. They were there to see Jean Harlow. But they were wasting their time. The newly widowed star didn't show. She was grieving in seclusion, heavily sedated.

Eliot pushed his way through to the entrance. He flashed his studio pass at the cops and at the sight of the magic letters M-G-M they let him through. Inside, the tiny anteroom was crowded. The only seating – sixteen high-backed wicker chairs – was already taken by the VIPs and the witnesses. Eliot joined the throng of reporters and photographers who crowded the aisles and the back.

In the second row sat Louis B. Mayer and Irving Thalberg. On Mayer's side was a worried-looking watchful man wearing a striped tie. Later Eliot discovered who he was: Ralph Blum, an M-G-M attorney. Sitting behind Thalberg was another shark-faced individual. Eliot recognised him: Martin Greenwood, the studio's business manager.

The Coroner came in with an assistant and the inquest began.

The first witness was Jean Harlow's stepfather, Marino Bello. Occupation mining. *Mining?* Had Eliot misheard? Was it perhaps *miming*?

A sleek charmer. Oil dripped from his hair, his skin, his words.

Bello testified he was not present at the time of Paul Bern's death. He didn't hear about it until around 9pm that Monday. He stated that his stepdaughter's marriage was a happy one.

Next: John Herman Carmichael, chauffeur and butler to the deceased. A plain, heavily-set man with a lumpy prize-fighter's nose. The dutiful and discreet servant.

He stated that Mrs Bern came home between 7 and 8pm, having finished her work at the studio. About an hour later he drove Jean Harlow to her mother's house for dinner. As she left she said to her husband: 'In case you don't come over, good night, dear.' Mr Bern replied: 'Well, I will be seeing you, dear.' The couple parted amicably. There was no quarrel of any sort.

Carmichael returned to 9820 Easton Drive the next morning, with his wife, who worked as Bern's housekeeper. She went to the kitchen to make coffee. Carmichael went on through the house and found his employer. 'It was quite pitiful. He was laying in a puddle of blood.' The room was not disturbed in any way out of the ordinary. Paul Bern was a great reader. There were books laying on the bed and nothing more than that. The chauffeur ran and called Davis the gardener, asking him to come inside. Next he told his wife to phone Jean Harlow's mother. After about an hour Mr Selznik and Mr Thalberg arrived. After a few minutes the police were called.

The Coroner, Frank A. Nance: 'I was wondering if there was any unnecessary delay in the police being called. The records show that they were not called until about two-fifteen and that you discovered the body about eleven-forty-five. Do you know any reason for that delay?'

Carmichael: 'No sir, I do not.'

The Coroner moved on. Carmichael had no reason to believe his employer was unhappy, dissatisfied, nervous or suicidal. He never mentioned the topic of suicide.

Q. 'Did you know he had two guns?'

A. 'Yes, sir.'

Q. 'Was he in the habit of carrying a gun?'

A. 'Yes, sir.'

Q. 'Did he ever tell you why he carried his gun?'

A. 'No sir, he never mentioned the gun to me at all.'

The questions continued. The marriage seemed to be very happy. There was no obvious reason why Paul Bern should kill himself. He and Mrs Bern never quarrelled. He didn't complain of any illness.

Next witness: Winifred Carmichael, housekeeper. A thick-set, plain woman. A reliable kitchen slave. A dutiful wife. You could reply on Winifred. She wouldn't give anything away. Hers very definitely wasn't the mystery voice on Eliot's phone.

Mrs Carmichael said she knew of no reason why her employer should take his own life. He was a very reserved sort of man.

Next witness: Irving Grant Thalberg.

That middle name was a surprise to Eliot.

Thalberg was neatly turned out. Pleasant and smart. A skilful witness. The words carefully chosen.

Upon being informed of Bern's death he went out to the house with David Selznick. They arrived around one o'clock. Thalberg had then phoned the police within a few minutes of entering the house.

Q. 'Did he ever discuss the suicide problem with you as a scientific fact or in any way?'

A. 'Yes he did.'

Q. 'Did he ever mention that he might do that some time?'

A. 'Yes he did.'

Q. 'So far as the domestic relations between Mr Bern and his wife are concerned, do you know of anything in that that would constitute a reason for him wanting to take his own life?'

A. 'I don't know of anything directly. I have heard of lots of things but I don't know of anything.'

No further questions.

Next witness: Martin Greenwood, business manager, M-G-M. A big man. If he had things to hide, he hid them behind a screen of affability.

Greenwood said he went to the house. He wasn't sure exactly what time he got there – probably about half past two. He was there when the police arrived. He had no knowledge of any motive for suicide.

Next witness: Clifton Earl Davis, gardener and handyman.

Another bit part for a black man. He seemed nervous. He was deferential, anxious to please.

He confirmed that Carmichael had called him into the house to see the body. He had never heard his employer mention suicide. He had no knowledge of any domestic inharmony. He knew of no reason why Bern might have taken his own life.

Next witness: Harold Allen Garrison, bootblack at M-G-M and occasional driver for Mr Bern. Everybody on the studio lot knew 'Slickum'. He polished everybody's shoes. He was everybody's friend. One of those larger-than-life characters. An extrovert. He perpetually fizzed with wise-cracks. Eliot had always found him rather tiresome. But most people adored the creep. Apart from his clown's role at the studio, Slickum was Paul Bern's night chauffeur. Carmichael usually only did days.

Slickum testified that Paul Bern spoke of suicide 'quite often'. It was a biological inheritance. 'He said his mother had and his father – I think his grandmother or father – and it run the family, but he hoped he would never have to do it.' It was damning testimony. And damming. It blocked the flow of other explanations.

According to Slickum his passenger would every now and then say 'Life is hard' and he would clasp his arms and slide down in the car. Every now and then Paul Bern talked of suicide. 'He might have within the last two or three weeks, just slightly.'

The Coroner asked if he had ever seen any marital inharmony.

'Just hugging and kissing all the time, just makes me mad.'

Q. 'There never was any quarrel?'

A. 'Never.'

On the Sunday night he had driven Bern home after collecting him from the Ambassador Hotel at 8.30pm.

Q. 'When you left him that night was he happy and cheerful?'

A. 'Just as usual.'

Q. 'Was he alone?'

A. 'Yes. Had to go about seventy-five stairs to his house and I would take the car home and I would watch there through the trees until he got in the house and then toot the horn and go home.'

Next witness: Blanche Williams, who had been Jean Harlow's personal maid for two years. Petite, young, nervous. Eliot leaned forwards, straining to hear.

Blanche knew of no reason why Mr Bern might want to kill himself. She saw very little of him. Mrs Bern was very happy with her husband.

Eliot relaxed. She wasn't the woman on the phone.

No further questions.

The Coroner: 'Is Mr Bern, the brother of the deceased here?'

Silence.

Not present.

'Is Mrs Paul Bern here?'

Silence.

The Coroner: 'I understand she is not. I have here a letter which I will read to the jury. It is from a doctor. *My dear Mr Nance, Miss Jean Harlow has been under my care since Monday, September 5th, 1932, and has been suffering a severe nervous collapse. Her appearance before the coroner's jury would severely endanger her life. Sincerely yours, Robert Helm Kenniscot.*'

Next witness: Detective Lieutenant Joseph Whitehead of

the Los Angeles City Division. He testified that he arrived at 9820 Easton Drive at two-thirty in the afternoon, fifteen minutes after getting the call from Irving Thalberg. The deceased was holding a .38-caliber Colt revolver, number 572972, firmly clasped in the right hand under the right side of the body. One shell was discharged, five bullets were still in the chamber. There were fingerprints on the gun but they were too faint to take a picture of, due to the fact there was oil on the gun. There was no sign that anyone had disturbed the position of the body or the room. There were no signs of a scuffle or anything of that sort. 'It was my conclusion it was suicide.'

A juror asked: 'Isn't it customary when one commits suicide that the gun falls by the side and does not stay in the hand?'

A. 'Not necessarily, no.'

Next witness: Detective Lieutenant F. Condaffer of the Los Angeles Police Department. He had found numerous bottles of pills in the house. None were labelled as narcotics.

Final witness: Dr Frank R. Webb, assistant autopsy surgeon of the Coroner's Office. A gunshot wound entered Paul Bern's right temple, two inches in front of his right ear. It went through the skull and brain, exiting on the left side of the head, two inches above the attached border of the left ear. The powder burns and the seared brain and shattered skull bones indicated a close proximity of the barrel of the gun at the time of the explosion. The wound was of a type seen in self-inflicted injuries.

The coroner asked the jury to determine whether the death of the deceased, Paul Bern, was suicidal, homicidal, accidental or natural.

The jury retired.

The jury returned with their verdict.

'Gunshot wound of head, self-inflicted by the deceased with suicidal intent at the home of the deceased, 9820 Easton Drive, West Los Angeles, California, motive undetermined.'

Eliot was one of the first to leave, borne out on a tide of running reporters. What was strange about the inquest, he thought, was that the note in Paul Bern's handwriting – what was surely a suicide note – had not been mentioned at all. And what about the mystery broad, Dorothy Millette? Where *was* she?

It wasn't worth going to the studio now. He drove home. He could work on the *Jacob's Room* treatment there. On the way he made a diversion to the bar off Wilshire, to see if Mildred was there in the darkness.

She wasn't.

But he saw her again that day – or rather that night. In his dream he was at the studio, sitting high up on the shoe polish stand. It was Slickum's stand but Mr Loquacity wasn't there.

Eliot realised to his horror that his clothes ended at the waist. He was wearing shoes but nothing on his legs. His underwear wasn't there. People were grinning as they walked by.

His condition was one of rigid excitement.

Mildred kneeled below him. She displayed a generous quantity of cleavage. Her left hand held a shoe brush. A blackened cloth rested in the palm of the other.

'I'm going to give you a good rubbing,' she chuckled. She reached up with the cloth.

But now he was no longer in the studio but standing in Yellowstone National Park. He was with twenty or so other people in an open rocky area. They were being addressed by a ranger in a green uniform. Eliot saw that though the others were clothed, he was completely naked.

'Regular as clockwork,' the ranger said. He pointed to an area behind him.

Eliot stepped forward and ran past the man, who shouted at him to come back. But it felt good to be dancing from rock to rock. A warm wind ruffled his hair. It was thrilling to be nude, every inch of him toasted by the sun.

Then the geyser erupted, squirting a hot whiteness, cone-shaped, expanding...

A tremendous sense of well-being flooded Eliot's body and he woke up.

Someone had tipped warm melted candle wax over his stomach.

'Mildred,' he whispered, as though she was beside him. But Mildred was not there. He was alone in the hot room. Somewhere a mile or so away the pulses of a siren rippled the skin of the sleeping city.

The night was like a chocolate egg with a soft, sticky treat inside, Eliot thought. A simile which, after the brusque application of a wet cloth and a brisk towel rub, led him into a strange dream involving a chocolate factory, an adulterous wife who looked like Mildred, and a man who mistook a tramp for his double.

# 6

*THAT EXTRAORDINARY WEEK was not yet over. And astonishing as it was, it was merely a prelude to the incredible events which were to follow.*

Eliot thought those two sentences would do rather nicely in *Of Flesh and Age*. He wrote them down in his notebook.

An omniscient author could know that the second sentence was true, whereas Eliot, trapped in the present, believed that nothing would ever equal the events of that extraordinary week.

They were not over yet because the next day, Friday September 9th 1932, was the day of Paul Bern's funeral. It was held at the Grace Chapel in Inglewood. Eliot decided to go and watch from a distance. So did two thousand other people. He managed to get near the front, so that he could see the chapel and the mourners as they arrived.

A vast heap of wreaths and flowers lapped the chapel walls like a many-colored snowdrift. They spilled down over the lawn.

And here they came – the cream of Hollywood! Eliot recognised quite a few sharks with glasses, as well as the moustache brigade, the executives, Thalberg and his film-star wife.

A sudden excitement rippled across the waiting crowd.

She had arrived!

The widow!

The platinum blonde herself!

Jean Harlow wore a long dark number trimmed with fur and a fetching black headscarf which drooped behind her neck, creating the slight suggestion of a nun. She looked pale and drugged. Her eyes stared down at the path, seeing nothing. She was supported by two men. The one to her right Eliot recognized from the inquest – her slippery Italian stepfather, Marino Bello. The other was a writer he was vaguely acquainted with – Willis Goldbeck. He'd talked to him a few times in the commissary. But it was the same with him as with the other writers – they were colleagues, not friends. They thought Eliot's fondness for serious fiction was a pointless self-indulgence. They were after stories that had hit potential. If there was passion there had to be guns, car chases, cops. They did not want Angst or unhappy endings, where good people die, or stare into space, broken by circumstance. They did not want Joycean reverie. A sentence should be short, with a sharp edge. They favoured monosyllables, wisecracks, crackling retorts. Keep the audience awake, alert, interested, amused, gripped, enthralled, stirred, throbbing, moved, happy. Let them go home feeling better than they'd done before the show started.

Goldbeck dropped back, leaving Marino Bello in charge of escort duties.

Sensation! As she drew closer to the chapel entrance Harlow began to weep. Suddenly there was a handkerchief in her hand, and a second one. Her face vanished into white cloth, which absorbed her salty spasms. Her stepfather glared at the crowd, as if holding it responsible for upsetting this broken woman.

Then all were inside and the doors closed. The ceremony began.

A section of the crowd drifted away.

Time dragged.

Occasional female wailings leaked out to entertain the restless onlookers. Finally a solitary violin could be heard, playing a lament.

Then, at last, the doors opened and out came Louis B. Mayer, who held on to Miss Harlow as one of his most precious assets. He guided his shining star to her night-black limo. A moment later the goddess was gone.

It was then, as the vast group of watchers began to disintegrate, that Eliot spotted Mildred. She was only about fifty yards away, standing close to the railings.

Excitedly, he pushed his way through the crowd. He needed to explain why he'd never come back on Monday. He guessed she was angry and hurt. He needed to make it up to her. He needed to tell her she'd been in his dreams.

'Mildred!'

She heard; turned; saw him.

A flicker of fear crossed her tense face. She swivelled, put her back to him. She began to run.

Eliot went in pursuit. He realised what it was. Mildred thought he was still mad at her for taking his Virginia Woolfs. And it was true – the loss of that signed copy of *The Waves* still rankled. But, heck – he wasn't going to press charges. He just wanted that particular volume back.

He ran, shoving people aside, mumbling *Sorry!* as they glared or cursed.

Had he seen this situation in a movie? Had he dreamed it? He needed to work it into his treatment of *Jacob's Room*. Jacob sees his girl in a crowd. He has to get to her before the cops do. He screams her name. But she knows the cops are watching her. Knowing that Jacob will never understand she desperately tries to flee. She knows that the closer Jacob gets, the more he's doomed. Finally he catches up with her. He seizes her arm.

'Jacob, baby – run! The cops have been tailing me for weeks.'

'I don't care. I had to see you again! I love you, you little fool. Don't you know that? I've always loved you!'

'Run, darling!'

Jacob runs.

But he's surrounded.

Jacob drops behind a car. He takes out his pistol and starts shooting. A cop drops, hit. A second one, a third...

Then the cops open up from all sides. Jacob is shot, repeatedly. His fallen body jerks with the impact of the slugs. His head drops. Close-up: there's a smile on his dead face.

His girl runs over, falls down, embraces the corpse. She kisses him. 'I'll love you until the end of time, baby!'

Then she snatches up his gun and starts popping at the cops. We see two of them fall. Then she is overwhelmed. She drops to the ground, shot through the heart.

High angle shot of the cops moving in from all sides to surround the dead bodies of the lovers.

Conundrum. End it there? Or should there be a final scene? Is there a risk this movie glamorizes crime and violence? Is there a need for a last shot with a priest chatting to a cop, conveying the message that crime-does-not-pay? Or does the double slaying say that anyway?

Food for thought!

Mildred disappeared from sight round the next junction. By the time Eliot reached it and followed the direction she'd taken she was gone. Maybe she'd grabbed a taxicab. Maybe she'd taken refuge in a bar. Maybe she was hiding up an alley.

He went looking but he didn't find her.

# 7

THAT WEEK WAS over.

Eliot spent the weekend smoking 127 cigarettes, drinking two bottles of bootleg Oklahoma sour mash corn whiskey and thinking firstly about Mildred and then about his next treatment. That first morning he went out to the Manderley store on the corner and bought some spaghetti, cheese and six apples. Back in his apartment he drank more whiskey. *The Waves* and *Jacob's Room* were done. Now he thought he'd have a crack at *Mrs Dalloway*.

The weekend was a blur. But out of it came some fine writing.

*Buster, I'll tell you two words that begin with D – defiance and death. And I don't just deal in the first of those two fine nouns!* [ shoots from his pocket, through the cloth of his raincoat ]

And later: *Sure I shot Sugar Reid. It was my way of communicating something he'd been waiting a long time to learn.*

The dialogue often came before the plot. That's how it was with Woolf. Her narratives had a tendency to wander. Her characters were too introspective. She'd never learned how important a car chase or a shoot-out is for grabbing attention. But that's not to say she didn't have something a scriptwriter couldn't use. The cinema was there – it just needed teasing out.

Eliot looked again at Woolf's feeble original and felt pretty damn pleased with himself. 'Death was defiance,' Miss Skinny wrote. 'Death was an attempt to communicate, people feeling the impossibility of reaching the centre which, mystically, evaded them; closeness drew apart; rapture faded;

one was alone.' Far too wordy. It was like the dame had her mouth stuffed with five sorts of candy. But there was potential there, definitely. The whole book had what it takes. It just needed improving.

*Let me tell you something, sister. Rapture fades. And one day you'll find yourself alone in a room with a worn carpet and a bill collector rapping at the door. And you'll look at yourself in the mirror and all you'll see is lines on your face that look like prison bars. And you'll think: I wish I'd said yes to Hank when I had the chance.*

A new week began. On the Monday he dropped off the two treatments at Thalberg's office. It wasn't until the Tuesday that Eliot heard the news. Harlow was back! At first they'd shut down filming *Red Dust* out of respect. Soon they'd quietly started up again, using a body double. But it turned out that Harlow had gotten bored of grief. She wanted action. Life wasn't about mooching around in your room brooding on the past. Hell, no! It was about getting out there and doing stuff. It's not love that makes the world go round. It's goddam honest to goodness *hard work*.

Clark was doing a scene with the double when Jean breezed in. She tapped the actress on the shoulder. 'Sorry, honey, the part's taken.'

*Action!*

But the studio saw a publicity angle. After the scene they had Jean go back to a stage doorway and stand in the frame. There was a smile on her purdy face and her right hand clasped her left rib cage, like she was struggling to hold back all the pain that swelled inside her. A mighty fine shot. And she's staring into the eyes of sweet Clark Gable, whose left hand is gripping the door knob – shaddup, doc – and whose right arm is stretched out in a gesture of welcome. *Come along in, princess. Your world is waiting for you.*

The next day a corpse was recovered from the Sacramento River. The decomposed remains were those of the elusive Dorothy Millette. Paul Bern's phantom old flame. The body went unclaimed. She was a has-been, a no one, a shadowy presence in the life of a dead man. There was no mileage in this story any more.

Next day Eliot received the invitation to a party in Beverly Hills, at the home of the director Millard Coleman. *Millard Coleman!* Eliot was baffled. Had there been a mistake? But there it was – an invitation card with his name on, all fancy copperplate, requesting his presence at Millard's home from four to six on Sunday.

As Eliot walked up to the house he could hear a live band performing 'Night and Day' in the garden. The house did not disappoint. The porch had been modelled on a temple in ancient Athens. The living room was long enough to get a light aircraft airborne. The marble stairs curving upwards beside the landing strip were the width of a Chevy Series AC International. Its banisters were caked in gold.

Outside, the patio was of similar dimensions. It could have hosted several tennis courts. The pool was Hollywood-standard. Its blue dancing waters stood between the house and a lawn that descended to a wall of tall, dense firs.

These sets were thronged with Millard Coleman's guests. Actors, producers, directors... Top people.

Millard stood just inside the porch, his wife at his side, welcoming each guest as they arrived. The director was a surprisingly short man, who wore shoes with specially raised heels. He was not yet thirty but he was already developing a paunch and growing another chin. His wife was tall, slender and beautiful. The standard Beverly Hills trophy wife.

Millard hugged, embraced, shook hands.

'Norma, darling!'

The reply was listened to and answered. 'That's great to hear! Hey, the drinks are over there, honey!'

'Clark, you old rascal – how goes it?'

The reply was listened to and answered. 'That's great to hear! Hey, the drinks are over there!'

Next: 'Spencer, you old rapscallion – how goes it?'

The reply was listened to and answered. 'That's great to hear! Hey, the drinks are over there!'

Next: 'Mickey! How goes it? How are the ears? Really? That's great to hear. Hey, the cheese is over there!'

Next: 'Balso Snell! How's the horse, you old devil! Really? Terrific! Hey, the drinks are over there!'

And then, finally, it was Eliot's turn. The director stared at him, puzzled, plainly struggling to identify him. The thin, towering wife-accessory was the silent movie actress Mary Lyons. She was one of the many who'd been annihilated by sound technology. Her voice was so soft it was virtually inaudible and no amount of coaching had been able to change that. The studio had dropped her. Luckily, by then she was married to Coleman. At that time she was the star and he was the new boy in town. Now their situation was reversed. She was a fading memory while his career went from success to success. Millard Coleman was good at making product that counted above all other considerations – terrific box-office returns.

Mary snatched the invitation card from Eliot's hand, glanced at it, and whispered in her husband's ear. She was only twenty-seven. She really was an extraordinarily beautiful woman, at least a foot taller than her husband.

Constructed from stale adjectives she somehow managed to appear fresh. Perfume stewed from rose petals and moonlight hung around her like a halo.

Millard beamed. 'Eliot Blunt, the writer! I'm truly, truly humbled you honoured us with your presence. How's it going, you genius you? Irving told me you'd given him two of the most dazzling treatments he's ever seen in all the time he's been in movies. *The Wolves* – what a title! Simple, yet gripping. And *Jacob: Gunman.* That socks a punch! Can't wait to direct them! Hey, friend, the drinks are over there!'

Eliot was dismissed. But as he moved away, Mary Lyons took hold of his hand. She stooped, put her lips close to his nearest lobule, and directed her soft message into his left ear canal. 'Come and see me later, when Mill has dealt with all the creeps. We need to talk.'

Astonished, Eliot nodded. What on earth could Mrs Coleman have to talk about with such a miserable nonentity as himself?

A thought occurred. Was she the woman on the phone? A thought instantly deleted. The woman on the phone had a louder, more distinctive voice.

Eliot headed for the nearest drinks table in a trajectory which was as straight as a slug sent by Jacob in his meanest mood. Champagne! Eliot consumed four glasses in succession and at once began to feel better about the condition of his world.

He went outside. It was important not to get too near the edge of the pool. Experience had taught him that unlimited supplies of free alcohol and a swimming pool are best kept at a distance.

'I'm completely pooped,' a fat man told him.

Eliot nodded solemnly. 'And I'm an amazingly competent

drunk,' he softly retorted.

The fat man looked at him as a bored biologist stares at an amoeba.

Eliot felt he should enlarge on that remark, to establish his regular guy status. 'I just want to drive out to Zabriskie Point and sit in my car and stare morosely out of the window at sand dunes,' he said. But the fat man had moved away to where white roses shone from a wall of trellis. Was that Elise Lay from Butte beside him? It looked like her. She seemed intoxicated. 'El largo adios!' she shouted at the Mexican maid, who was sweeping up the fragments of a broken green bottle which lay around her ankles. Then she saw Eliot. She made an obscene gesture involving two scarlet-tipped fingers and a thumb.

'I live for syntax,' he replied. 'Adeus, minha adorada!'

Next Eliot was at the far side of the pool. On his shaky, shivering walk there he had not fallen in. This was an achievement worth celebrating. There was a fellow bobbing at his elbow. He held a tray which was within reach, magnificently motionless and horizontal. Eliot took hold of a shallow circular glass in each hand. He handled them like an expert gunslinger.

'Here's how!' He raised his glass to a strange, beautiful redhead in a blue gown. She regarded him coldly and turned away.

'Down the rat hole!' he remarked to a blonde with magnificent cleavage, as he drained the companion glass. The blonde grinned and blew him a kiss.

But a moment later she'd evaporated.

The band was at one side of the smooth green turf, on a small stage. The singer – a black woman, well-built – was crooning 'All of Me'. She was really rather good, Eliot thought. She had a smoky, drawling voice that squeezed every last ounce of emotion out of the simplest words and expressions.

The song made him think of Mildred. It ripped him open, the strange sudden decay of that short ecstatic relationship. Inside his heart maggots thrived. He was still viewing them with scientific curiosity – little white things with curving backs, going about their work with great energy and excitement – when something took hold of an elbow. A force slowly spun him round. A person stood there, managing to remain vertical while California tilted a little and began to break free of the good ol' U. S. of A.

'Those two treatments,' the man said. 'I've never been so electrified.'

'Communism is Soviet power plus the electrification of the whole country!' Eliot replied, or felt he'd replied, though possibly he'd never opened his mouth.

'Are there more?' the man asked.

'*Mrs Dalloway*,' Eliot said. 'A woman who transformed herself by night!'

'Get it to my office when it's finished. I can't tell you how excited I am.'

Eliot realised he was talking to Irving Thalberg. The great man's mouth writhed and words slithered out. 'How did you get on with the dame on the phone?'

'Nowhere, sir. Been everywhere. Haven't heard her voice. Not in stores or speakeasies or the commissary. Not nowhere, sir.'

'Well keep trying, Eliot.'

'I surely will, sir.'

Several trays later he was inside the house, talking to his host's wife, Mary. She gazed at him with fierce affection.

Evidently he was making perfect sense.

'I'm a tired and disappointed woman,' she confided. 'I'm no bargain for anyone. But I need someone to be kind to me.'

'You've got guts and honesty. You can tell anybody to go to hell, including me.'

Her eyes narrowed. 'I think you've already been there.'

Along the edge of this shimmering speech and counter-speech a number of millipedes were playing a game of can't-catch-me. How they hopped and skipped, like tiny flakes of burnt paper blown on the wind! Some were little more than eyelashes.

Eliot felt sure he'd read this dialogue before, in a deleted scene. But which scene?

'So you see,' he explained in a voice that had speeded up to keep pace with the millipedes, 'Mrs Dalloway is a woman who has two sides to her character. By day she's a respectable wife, arranging the running of her household. But when night falls, her true self emerges. Her husband is often away – or asleep by ten-fifteen. It's then that she slips out of the house. All she's wearing is a skimpy black dress and a pair of black leather gloves. No underwear. She likes to feel the cool night air caress her like a lover...'

Mary Lyons emitted the faintest of sighs.

'We see her climbing a drainpipe. The shocking truth emerges. Mrs Dalloway is the Black Panther! She's the infamous burglar who's been stealing jewellery from homes across the city. The police have been seeking the Panther for months. They set traps – but she always outwits them.'

'Oh my God,' Mary breathed. 'Is your body as exciting as your mind?'

Eliot wasn't sure what to say. But he didn't need to talk. She did the dialogue for both of them.

'The thing is,' she whispered. 'Millard has a woman in Santa Monica. And another one in Santa Barbara. There's even a bitch in Santa Rosa.' She paused. 'Christmas is hell for me. Pure hell.' Her eyes were pools of resentment mixed with longing, where thin starved goldfish swam with an aching slowness.

Eliot squeezed her hand. 'You poor baby. He's such a fool.'

She stared at him. 'My God, you're so handsome, so intelligent, so wise.' Her perfume enveloped Eliot like a sweet fog. The afternoon was becoming a little blurry in every dimension, every aspect, every sweet trembling nuance.

It was hard for Eliot to know what to say in response to this beautiful, shrewd, clever woman. It was like she'd said 'Two and two make four' or 'The earth is warmed by the sun' or 'What Louis B. Mayer wants, Louis B. Mayer gets.'

A silence began. It might have brought a chill, or even ice, or the slow thrusting tongue of a glacier, but figurative possibility was snuffed out by an exciting new development in the plot. The guests, who one moment were talking intently, creating the Niagara roar of a hundred concentrated liquor-oiled conversations, stopped dead in mid-sentence. The singer broke off singing 'Please' and fell silent.

Something sensational had happened.

Jean Harlow had arrived! The sexquisite Harlow! The alabaster outlaw! The new kinda gotcha' girl!

Millard was there, back in position at the entrance. He had put his arms around Harlow and placed his dry narrow lips briefly against her powdered right cheek. When his face withdrew a fine white dust like chalk lay upon his mouth and the tip of his nose. It gave him the appearance of a ghost – or perhaps a clown.

Mary was there too, to Eliot's surprise, welcoming Harlow

and her entourage. The director's wife had somehow transported herself from his side and moved there without any passage of time occurring. What a magical woman she was, he thought, and two dozen millipedes paused their game to nod in animated agreement. Mary moved with grace, not restrained by the petty limitations of gravity, geography or time.

Now the formalities had been dispensed with. The effusiveness with which Harlow had been welcomed diminished as the Colemans worked their way down the hierarchy of the gang of hangers-on. Mama Jean had to be given the full huggy-kissy treatment because, after all, she was the power behind the throne. It was also necessary to embrace that awful Italian she'd married. But the others – they were only worth the briefest of handshakes. They were studio writers. For some unknown reason Harlow liked to cultivate these creeps.

Eliot felt a pang of jealousy. He recognised several of them. Some of them had screenplay credits on recent successful movies. And then the Harlow crowd moved on, into the main body of the party. They vanished from sight. The band struck up. The colored woman was doing a lively version of 'It Don't Mean a Thing'. It was as though she'd recharged the party's rundown engine. The volume of the conversation grew and grew. Actresses were shrieking with laughter. A bottle fell to the ground and shattered – much hilarity. There were girls in the pool, screaming. Now they were topless. A man in a suit jumped in to join them.

*Doo wah, doo wah, doo wah, doo wah...*

Eliot staggered to the john. It was vast inside. A chamber of white tiles, mirrors on every wall, gold taps. The mirrors meant he could watch himself from every angle. A hundred

Eliots stood there, receding into the distance. He swayed and unbuttoned. His bladder was swollen with a pint or two of champagne. Bubbles fizzed in his flesh. He felt weightless. He seemed to float. The jet was the color of water. He stood there for twenty minutes, admiring the perfection of the arc. He adjusted his aim. Or was it less than that? Only ten? Someone was thumping on the door. The knocking on the door! The porter attends the gate. The Scotch play. Scotch. It was time to go. There'd surely be some decent hootch at the bar, n'est-ce pas? Maybe even some vintage Old Forester...

Hic! Tee hee!

'You sure took your time buddy,' a blue jacket attached to a yellowish pockmarked scowling potato may have said as Eliot drifted back to the runway. In his experience that sour kind of citizen was often on the other side of the door when a fellow was relaxed and taking his time.

The band outside brought 'Dinah' to an end and there was a spitter-spatter of applause. A pitter-patter. A splittle-splattle. A tinkle-winkle. Eliot found himself drinking a cocktail the color of a rainbow, weedy with sprigs of drowned mint, inside which a sliver of peach lay as motionless as a dead goldfish. Time seemed to pass, and he had the impression of holding a number of brief fragmentary conversations with strangers. Then everything started to disintegrate. People were thanking Millard for a truly wonderful party, guests were collecting their coats from the maids in the room off the entrance hall. But this shouldn't be happening, Eliot felt. This wonderful day must not be allowed to end.

'Wait!' he shouted in a loud, piercing voice that paralysed the room. Was it the gorgon who turned people to stone? Eliot had that effect.

He stepped forward, to the centre of the space that was created for him. He was aware of some seventy or eighty people staring at him with acute curiosity.

'Let me round off this marvellous, marvellous and splendid, splendid time we've all had here today with a short recitation.'

Puzzlement; wonder; mild amusement.

Eliot pressed his right hand against his left breast and began. He gave it his Shakespearean best.

Oh! My love is like a red, red rose
that's newly sprung in June,
Oh! Oh!
My love, my love
is like the melody
that's sweetly played in tune.

Oh!
So fair you are, my gorgeous gal
so deep in love am I,
that I will love you like a pal
until the ocean's dry.

Oh yes!
Until the ocean's gone my dear,
and the rocks melt in the sun,
I will love you, oh, my dear,
while the sands of time shall run.

Oh fair thee well, you gorgeous gal,
or stay behind with me your pal,
and we will share so many smiles
on a trip that lasts ten thousand miles.

Eliot stepped back to indicate that the performance was over. He delivered a modest half-nod and granted his audience the warm beam of an artist who knows that today of all days he has reached the very summit of his artistry.

A silence hung over the Coleman residence. Eliot felt it was exactly like the emotional shock which stuns an audience, rendering it mute, in those long lingering seconds after the uttering of 'Go, bid the soldiers shoot,' or when the curtain comes down on fat, flushed Donna Elvira and her associates, or when the perspiring musicians let their instruments drop to their laps after completing a scorching, frenzied, utterly brilliant performance of String Quartet No. 16 in F major.

Or was it?

Eliot waited for the applause.

The silence seemed to expand and grow colder.

Millard Coleman glared at Eliot from an ashen face. At the back of the crowd Irving Thalberg's face wore an expression of deep unhappiness. One of the vaguely familiar studio writers grinned, winked, and made a throat-cutting gesture with his forefinger.

And then a voice – an assertive female voice – said: 'That was the most gosh-darned beautiful thing I ever did hear in all my life!'

The crowd parted.

A goddess moved to the front.

She stood there, resplendent, curvaceous, imperial. Trembling.

*Jean Harlow.* All 105 pounds of her. The champagne hair cascading down, framing that gorgeous impudent tomboyish sensual slightly plump face with the pencil eyebrows and the piercing blue eyes. She sobbed the words out: 'That was just so – so beautiful.' She seemed on the brink of tears.

Harlow raised her arms. She began to clap.

Suddenly the entire room was applauding furiously. 'Bravo!' shouted the cut-throat writer, giving a thumbs-up gesture.

'Terrific!'

'Sensational!'

'Wow!'

When the thunder of approval had ceased Mary Lyons piped up. 'You're so wonderful, Eliot, you should go into acting!'

'That's right!' someone agreed. 'Watch out Clark!'

There was warm laughter. Gable – a good sport – gave a cheery wave.

Then Millard spoke. He was genial, delighted, comforted, and very, very happy. 'Thanks for coming, folks. And thanks to Ellis here for wrapping things up in such a memorable way.'

'Eliot,' Eliot said.

But no one heard him. They were all leaving now. He heard the sharp click of starters engaging motors. He heard the sputter of primitive internal combustion engines bursting into action.

'Don't worry about *him*,' Mary said, gripping his arm. 'He doesn't matter. But *you* do.'

Harlow was leaving too. But as she left she turned and blew Eliot a kiss. Her entourage supported it with waves, cheers, and cries of 'Sensational!' and 'Genius!'

But Eliot wasn't paying much attention, now. He swayed a little; closed his eyes. Bright scarlet semi-colons danced across the darkness.

His head hurt, he was drunk, a hangover using drills and hammers seemed to be making a premature bid for his attention, and now he knew who the woman was who'd spoken to him on the telephone while he dreamed of a back door and a series of receding panels.

All along he knew that voice had seemed vaguely familiar. He shivered at this strange and perplexing knowledge.

*It was Jean Harlow who'd called him on the phone that morning!*

# 8

BY MONDAY ELIOT WAS on the mend. He'd vomited a few times, drunk several gallons of hot black coffee sweetened with honey, eaten seven boiled eggs, and imbibed a pint of orange juice. He was fragile and there was a trembling in his fingers but he was basically able to function. He'd been here before. He'd survive.

Once on the M-G-M lot he headed straight for Thalberg's office. He was kept waiting for over an hour but that was just fine. His head tipped forwards and he dozed under his homburg. The last drops of alcoholic excess quietly evaporated from his tender, delicate, sensitive flesh. All he was aware of now was a delicate faraway throbbing which might have been inside his head or could just have been a studio pump doing something with water the other side of the nearest sound stage. He remembered a rejected scene he'd written where women prisoners escaped down a big drainage pipe, shooting out of the end into the countryside and freedom. Maybe they were using it after all.

Footsteps passed to and fro as more important people than Eliot entered and left Thalberg's office. Stars, money-men, directors. Eliot did not like waiting rooms. They reminded him of dentists, doctors and hairdressers.

At last the great man appeared in his office doorway and called him in.

Thalberg snatched eagerly at the *Mrs Dalloway* treatment which Eliot held out to him. The producer said quietly: 'If it's as good as those other two... You have a real gift, you know, Eliot.'

'Thank you, sir.'

Then Eliot told him his great discovery.

'Jean Harlow, eh?' Thalberg said dully. He didn't appear surprised. He fell silent. Finally he said: 'Any idea how she got your number?'

'I don't think she did, sir.'

Eliot explained. In her distress the actress had plainly misplaced a digit. She hadn't meant to phone him at all.

Thalberg looked relieved. 'That figures.' He stood up. He seemed transfigured by a sudden joy. 'Well, keep this to yourself, Eliot. Let's let sleeping alligators have their rest down there in the Mississippi mud amid the pine forests and the silent phlegmatic hamlets where simple folk grow mushrooms and make incompetent whiskey. It's all water under the Tallahatchie Bridge now. What's done is done. It's all over now, Bubba Blue.' Thalberg extended his hand. The meeting was over. 'What next with Woolf?' he enquired as Eliot headed for the door.

'Another neglected little number no one's picked up on. *Orlando.*'

'Set in the States! You never mentioned this dame wrote American fiction!' Thalberg grinned. 'Heck, I thought she was a limey like you. I never realised she was a yankee.'

Eliot corrected Thalberg's preposterous assumptions.

On the drive home that day he called in at Connie Feshun's *Just-Fried Diner*. The Scotch eggs there were unique, sumptuous, tremendous. It was there he fell into conversation with a dour preacher, Jimmy Hogg. But this has no bearing on the story which is being told and so this paragraph need go no further nor give birth to narrative piglets with a duty to scamper and grow fat.

That evening Eliot did a little work on *Of Flesh and Age*. He came up with a terrific ending for a chapter: *I went to bed full of whiskey and frustration and dreamed about a man in a bloody Chinese coat who chased a naked girl with long jade earrings while I ran after them and tried to take a photograph with an empty camera.*

That night, after emptying a quarter of a bottle of fraudulent Old Forester, Eliot tottered off for his night's rest. He dreamed that he was lying naked on the bed. Mildred, dressed in a suit of armour, leaned over him with a large screwdriver. It had a red handle. He was surprised to see that the lower part of his body consisted of a pinkish slab covered in protuberances the size and shape of toadstools. Mildred was slashing at these lumps, hacking them off, one by one. There was no pain or blood. Once she was done, Eliot's lower body shimmered and he re-grew his legs and genitals.

Now he was in his roadster, still naked, alone, heading up Laurel Canyon. To his surprise the car turned off the road and went bouncing up a wide stairway, which he recognised as the one in Millard Coleman's home. At the top the roadster turned left and went down a dark passageway. The ground became squelchy and muddy, with flame-shaped weeds pressed against the walls. In a sudden spectacular burst of sunlight the corridor opened out into a brightly lit plain containing many Red Indians. They sat cross-legged, smoking long slender pipes. The car passed them and slowed beside a small house with an open window. Eliot climbed in through it. There, in an empty room, a huge naked woman sat at a grand piano playing 'It Don't Mean a Thing'. On the top of the piano lay a copy of H. Rider Haggard's *She*. The pianist turned to greet him, her vast breasts flopping like sacks of water. The room whacked him with a stench which reminded Eliot of a long pier railed with white two-by-fours thirty miles up the coast highway. The fat pianist had red lipstick around her mouth. As she opened it Eliot saw that she had no teeth. Drool gushed from the corners of her huge smile. 'You come along in, right now!' she cried.

Next morning Eliot went back to that *Of Flesh and Age* chapter ending. He deleted it. He saw now that it was too simplistic, too implausible, too feverish and over-written. It read like a sentence composed by a man who'd been drinking too much.

He headed to the studio and spent the morning in his office working on *Orlando*. The thing was to find the right angle. He figured it would be about an actress – a screen goddess. She was in love with a pilot. But she had a terrible secret. She was five hundred years old. She was a vampire! She'd been around in Shakespeare's time. She'd wowed the Globe crowd with her Ophelia, her Juliet, her Lady Macbeth. Of course back then she'd had to pretend to be a boy. And now she had a terrible dilemma. She fed off the blood of young men. How could she marry her true love when his neck was so irresistible?

Eliot needed a few tumblers of Old Forester to crack open that puzzle. He was just starting work on the third slug of amber inspiration when the door was thrown open.

It was Mary Lyons.

'We don't have much time,' she said. She turned the key in the lock and crossed to the blinds, flicking them down.

She had her clothes off inside ninety seconds and stood before him, tall, exquisitely shaped, suntanned, with small firm breasts. She kept her shoes on – little black numbers with high heels. She leaned against the wall in the corner.

'Quick!' she hissed. 'Hurry. We've got fifteen minutes max. Maybe only ten.'

Eliot undid his belt.

She evidently wanted a knee-trembler. Fine by him. He

stood against her, his fingers sliding like snakes around her many attributes – breasts, thighs, slippery hairy perfumed crevices – while her own rough, hungry reptiles concentrated on his unripe leathery plums and his fully-inflated tube of desire. Soon, like railroad carriages, they were connected, and she was grinding herself against him, muttering to herself in that faint whispery voice of hers. He had difficulty deciphering her monologue but what little he could understand sounded like it used repeatedly a pair of consonants – the fifth and the tenth of the alphabet – and the fifth vowel. Finally she arrived at the fourth vowel, a sequence, rising and falling in volume. As he maintained his steady rhythm Eliot recalled John Aubrey's story about Walter Raleigh and the Maid of Honour. She was up against a tree in a wood and seemed at first boarding to be fearful of her honour. 'Nay, sweet Sir Walter!' the Maid cried, and then, as the danger and the pleasure grew higher, she cried out, 'Swisser Swatter, Swisser Swatter!' A thought which, as his momentum began to speed up, led him to remember the First Folio of 1623 and its record of the final ejaculation of the Prince of Denmark: O,O,O,O.

Mary pushed him away, mopped herself with a handkerchief, then dressed. 'Not bad,' she whispered. At first Eliot took this as a compliment about his ignescent performance but then he saw that she was looking at her silver wristwatch. 'Seven minutes,' she said. 'That's pretty good.'

Then she was at the door, unlocking it. 'I must go. Millard will be looking for me.'

She disappeared from the chapter.

Eliot waited ten minutes then went to the commissary for coffee and a sandwich.

\*

*A wild and open moor. Orlando has a steel-blue feather in her cap. We see rooks whirl across an empty sky. Orlando trips and breaks her ankle. She attempts to get up, screams in pain, and collapses. She lies there, helpless. Time passes. The hooves of a horse are heard. Its rider comes crashing across the moor. At the last moment he swerves to avoid Orlando. He springs down. Clark Gable's moustache bends with tender anxiety. 'You are hurt!'*

*Orlando smiles up at him. 'No, sir, I am dead.'*

Eliot frowned. Woolf was utterly hopeless at names. You couldn't possibly have Clark playing a character called Marmaduke Bonthrop Shelmerdine. That was a pansy name. The character needed robust American nomenclature, full of prime red meat.

A pint of bogus Old Forester, Eliot decided, would help him locate it.

Glug,

glug,

glug.

Bud.

Bud Hardberger.

Buzz...

Buzz Ekker.

Dave...

Dave Phak.

Byron Deckard.

Ray Cassidy.

And then he found it. The sun broke through the clouds. Its beams shone like première searchlights. The celestial chorus went full volume.

*Bud Winger.*

That was perfect for a pilot.

Eliot finished off the whiskey. He felt just fine – damned fine. His internal heating was in tip-top condition. A glow of good cheer warmed his stomach and every atom of his being. He pulled up the blinds that Mary had closed. His small plaster bust of Shakespeare, usually very serious, deep in thought, had a change of mood. It beamed back at him as it turned to pure gold. Gosh yesh! Ish jesht you and me, Will!

Through the cracked window Eliot could see the pink Pacific sun as it ebbed into a soft, layered mist where violet and indigo lay with shimmering cobalt and bright magenta. It seemed to exist in that zone where headaches and hangovers experimented with color.

Hell, yes.

It was time to quit for the day.

As he gazed at the sky's spectacular underside he reflected that every writer should possess not only a dictionary and a thesaurus but also a tint chart.

That night he dreamed a blonde woman in green crêpe had invited him inside her house, leading him to a brown-and-red room with a lot of books in it. On a desk lay a scholarly paper by Victor Tausk. The blonde woman said she had to go out and invited Eliot to stay there and read Tausk's piece. It concerned a man's dream of seeing a former governess in a dark dress which fitted very tightly across her buttocks. The article concluded that this illustrated how lewd and lustful the governess was, the filthy, teasing little slut. Eliot went to the window. A square white garage stood obscenely in the rear of the house. Next there was the spurting squeal of abruptly applied automobile brakes. The blonde woman rushed into the room. She was naked, apart from her high-heeled scarlet shoes. Her face was white, her eyes jet black.

'My husband won't be home tonight,' she whispered. Eliot saw that she was Mary Lyons.

He went eagerly towards her but found himself stepping out on to the stage of Carnegie Hall. He was wearing a white tie and tails. His ebony shoes shone in the twin spotlights. Eliot bowed at the thunderous applause. He displayed his palms to quieten his hundreds – thousands! – of ardent fans. 'Ladies and gentlemen... I give you... Mozart's Piano Sonata number twelve, in F Major.'

He sat down at the grand piano. He adjusted the height of his stool. He cleared his throat. He raised his hands, just like Nosferatu. Eliot saw that he needed to trim his fingernails.

Horror! His fingers refused to function!

The audience stared in puzzled silence, then grew restless.

Suddenly Eliot's piano teacher strode on to the stage and reproached him for neglecting to practise. He was followed by the hairy Austrian with the cigar. 'Your sexual abstinence imposes itself on you by a severe neurosis,' the doctor said. 'As for your repeated dreams of going upstairs with your mother... Your compulsive self-restraint is damaging. May I recommend... '

In the orchestra pit a man wearing a Venetian carnival mask raised a giant pair of cymbals. He brought them fiercely together. A piercing thunderous ringing metallic crash distributed headaches across the audience. Then silence.

Eliot didn't see the gunman in the Dress Circle, he just heard the shot. Freud dropped to the floor, bleeding copiously from the groin. Half a gallon of blood gathered like beetroot soup between his pin-striped legs. Freud's right hand clawed at the mess, desperately reaching for something.

The architecture changed. It was no longer Carnegie Hall

but a dark apartment on Laverne Terrace. The shadow of a eucalyptus tree lay on the wall like something big and evil and hungry. A blue-haired man stood in a doorway, holding a big purple gun in his small grey greasy hands. Behind him stood an angry red-faced man with a scarred cheek. Staring over his shoulder was a smirking loose-mouthed chinless man with a green pallor who said his name was Marmaduke. Behind these three characters was a mirror, in which Eliot saw himself. He looked jaundiced. As he continued to stare at himself the mirror shattered. The dream had closed for the night. Sleep was now a dark featureless river, floating him onward to the golden beginning of a fresh Californian morning.

# 9

MUCH LATER ON, ELIOT realised that 1932 was the best year of his life.

He just didn't know it at the time.

It was two days later and the *Orlando* treatment was pretty much wrapped up. He'd delivered the others to Thalberg's redhead. She didn't seem to remember him.

Eliot decided to have a quiet evening in with a bottle, some bennies, and the Empress of the Blues. He'd drink a toast to the Oxford comma.

Velvet twilight turned to warm night. Under the soft street lights below he could see tiny swarms of punctuation dancing to and fro. Hyphens swooped excitedly around semi-colons like a dogfight in *Hell's Angels*. Then a passing pair of parentheses scared them off.

Someone knocked softly at the door. Three urgent knocks.

Eliot brushed cigarette ash from his shirt and went to see who it was.

A woman wearing dark glasses; a blonde woman, doing her best to look like Jean Harlow; a woman who looked from side to side, jerkily, nervously, like a bird; a woman with a dead fox draped around her shoulders; a woman who slid past Eliot, hurriedly closing the door; a woman whose appearance in his apartment triumphantly reasserted the merits of the semi-colon, a punctuation mark which first appeared in all its frabjous originality in the first edition of *De Aetna ad Angelum Chabrielem Liber* – a book, in part, about summer snow. *Summer Snow*. What a terrific title! Once he'd got *Of Flesh and Age* finished, he'd give it a go. With a title like that it had to be a love story. A delicate coming-of-age story. Young man, older woman. Young girl, older man. Innocence and experience. But nothing dirty – not if it hoped to be optioned...

'Honey, are you going to offer me a drink? I sure could use one.' The woman had taken her glasses off and was staring around the room.

'Jeepers creepers! You really *are* Jean Harlow!' The dimple, the weird eyebrows, the oddly unreal metallic color of the hair...

Harlow chuckled and nodded. 'My, what a lot of books you have!'

It was true. He was drowning in books. And he had lots of good stuff – up to date, cutting-edge. *Sanctuary*. *The Apes of God*. *The Murder at the Vicarage*. *Vile Bodies*. *Tarzan the Invincible*.

'Old Forester okay? It's probably not the real thing but it tastes okay.'

'A simulacrum of Old Forester would be just swell.'

By the time she'd slipped off her coat and thrown it over a chair Eliot had the glasses filled.

'Here's to it.'

She nodded, gulped the liquor down. 'Listen, honey. I owe you an apology. Phoning you up like that. It wasn't fair. It was just that at that moment in my life I needed to reach out to someone – and the only person I could think of was you. I guess that sounds crazy, you being a stranger and all. Let me explain.'

She rested a hand on his arm, then jerked it away, as if she'd touched a hot iron. Something had exploded somewhere nearby. It made her react convulsively, like a troubled veteran of the trenches. The piercing boom was followed by a long stuttering crackle. Out there, someone was having a fireworks party. A scream cut through the darkness and there was some brief jagged laughter.

Harlow cracked her knuckles. From nowhere she'd conjured a cigarette. With a shaky hand she inserted it between her plump scarlet lips. Eliot moved forward and produced fire. He held the pale sinuous flame close, keeping it in position as she sucked. When it was lit she kicked off her pumps.

She wandered around the room, fidgety and restless. 'Hey, that's a swell torchiere!'

The palm of her free hand lightly brushed the smooth torso of the lamp and made its way very slowly in the direction of the tip, which held a leaf-shaped bulb. Harlow released a tiny moan that endured longer than seemed proper. 'I haven't seen one quite this big before,' she breathed.

Two fingers of her other hand held the cigarette between her lips and she drew on it, exhaling. Eliot watched the grey smoke drift across to the high dark corner where a spider sometimes stayed. The smoke grew smaller, like the memory of an ancient love, until finally it dissolved. Harlow stubbed out the cigarette in a tub holding a wrinkled cactus. She emitted a jittery laugh. 'Sorry, sweetheart. I'm a bag of nerves. They watch me all the time. They try to control me.'

Eliot was shocked. 'Who does?'

'The whole shebang. Momma. That wop creep she married. The studio. Louis, Irving... They want to be sure their product won't let them down. No public embarrassments, huh. No scandal. No unsuitable men.' She looked at Eliot foxily. 'Are you an unsuitable man?'

'I do hope so. I hope so very much.'

'Listen, I called you about Paul because – well, we'd had a disagreement. He left me feeling worthless. I said terrible things. I said I wished he'd drop dead! And then see what happened... ' She began to sob.

Eliot slipped an arm around her. 'Hey, Jean, honey. Don't blame yourself.'

'Oh but I do!'

Her big eyes seemed to swell and become more circular, like those of a large insect. A scenario flashed in Eliot's mind like studio lightning. *Devil Girl from Pluto*. Harlow in a leather outfit, with a black cloak. Her space ship develops engine trouble and crashes in the desert. Clark Gable comes to her assistance. They fall in love. But it cannot be. 'Ours can only ever be a Plutonic love, dearest, because – '

Harlow's bug eyes stared through Eliot, as if he was made of glass or some random specks of punctuation which had come together magnetically to make a name. *Eliot*. He had the odd thought that that he was merely an assemblage of hyphens attached to colons, with a solitary free-floating period. He was invented, fake, a puppet, while Harlow was electrifyingly alive. She exuded soft feminine odours, powdery and dry and musky and delightful. Her eyes, which had contracted and become human again, now enlarged themselves once more. He sensed she was looking out into the darkness of the night, the darkness of the world, that dark beating smoking core which burns unseen beyond the page. Eliot felt intoxicated. None of this seemed real. It was like one of those stories *The Saturday Evening Post* liked to publish. There would be a surprise at the end of this charming and romantic scene. The plot would do a melancholy somersault. It would turn out that she'd mistaken him for the poet who'd written that god-awful, over-rated, name-dropping, interminable poem which everybody liked to pretend they liked but which no one – no one at all! – understood. And she'd finally be revealed as a

Jean Harlow impersonator from a business that catered for people who wanted to add a comic spark to their evening's entertainment. Ezra Pound had paid.

'It wasn't your fault,' Eliot whispered tenderly.

'You can't know that. It was what Paul said that hurt. And until you've seen it – you can't know – you can't possibly understand.'

Eliot had no idea what she was talking about.

'That's a gorgeous perfume,' he remarked, inhaling the fragrance that seemed to surround her like the as-yet undiscovered Van Allen belt. 'It must be French.' He took a few quick sniffs around her ears. 'My God! It's Brise Ambrée!'

'Oh Eliot! You're so knowledgeable!'

He nodded, shyly, and smiled, knowingly. In fact he'd read about her fondness for this brand in *Photoplay*. But she didn't need to know that.

Now they were sitting companionably together on the davenport. Harlow was wearing one of those long silver numbers that went from her clavicle to her ankles. The twinkling fabric clung to her curves.

'The guys told me you were a little screwy but no one else reads as many books as you. They said you had a fine taste in fiction.'

'The guys?'

'The writers I hang out with on the lot. But others have confirmed it. Irving says he's really excited by the treatments you're doing. He reckons *Bring Me The Head of Jacob Flanders* is gonna be *huge*. And he loves *The Dalloway Woman*. Comedy genius! As for *Waves of Blood*. Irve says he's truly, truly humbled by it.'

'But – '

'Woops!' Harlow released a peal of laughter. 'He told me not to tell you he'd changed the titles. He says you writers can be awful touchy about things like that.'

'They're not my titles! They're Virginia Woolf's!'

'Whatever. Say, my glass seems to be empty.'

'We can do better,' Eliot smiled. He went to the panelled section of the paragraph where he kept his special liquor and returned with two champagne cocktails.

'Chin chin!'

'Absolutely!'

'Here's to it!'

'Down the hatch!'

Harlow snuggled up to him. 'Say it to me. Say that poem you recited at Millard's party.'

'If you really want me to... '

Her free hand crawled up his thigh. 'I do. I very definitely do.'

'Okay, sweetheart.' His heart thumped. Eliot cleared his throat and began.

'Oh my lurve is like a red, red rose that's newly sprung in June, oh my luff is like the melody that's sweetly played in tune, so fair you are, my frabjous gal, so deep in love am I, I'm gonna love you like a pal until the ocean's dry, oh yes, yes, yes, until the ocean's gone my dear, and the rocks melt in the sun, I'll love you, love you, love, dear while the sands of time shall run, so fare thee well, you gorgeous gal or stay behind with me your pal, and we will share so many smiles on a trip that lasts ten thousand miles... '

'Oh baby... '

Convulsively Harlow threw herself on him. Her hand moved over the neighbourhood of his pants where that damned uncontrollable needy impatient pleading pressured blood-packed ridiculous organ pushed itself against white cotton, straining to be free. Eliot hoped she hadn't noticed the tiny yellow teardrop down there, where the little fellow had sobbed in his sleep.

A moment later both her hands were applying themselves to the hem of her dress. She peeled the garment off. It was true what they said, Eliot saw.

No underwear. Not up there, where her pale magnificent brown-eyed breasts gazed at him invitingly. And not down there, either.

Harlow stretched herself out on the davenport. Her smooth gorgeous stupendous thighs moved apart, reminding him of a bridge he'd once seen, mechanically bifurcating before an approaching yacht with a very tall mast. Wasn't that in Madison County? Uncertainty and forgetfulness ate like rust at his past. A fog lay across ambiguous stretches there, which no biographer would ever disperse.

Her shrubbery was pure platinum. It was well-fertilised wire, a little on the wild side. It was like a Christmas decoration. It brought a mood of celebration and joy to the proceedings. Its glitter and good humour brought thoughts of that sonnet exposing conventional simile and metaphor as risible when contrasted with the earthy reality of woman. That adjective *dun* for mammaries had rather fallen out of fashion. Now it was all diluted sepias and varieties of burnt umber and banal shades of autumn brown.

'I haven't – ' she ejaculated. 'Not for weeks and weeks. Oh God.' Her hands fluttered, sketching absent butterflies.

Then, abruptly, they were embracing like territorial crustaceans, locked rigidly together. Her hair smelled faintly of ammonia. Her breasts arched and trembled with a kind of shivering sob. She gasped. She groaned. These last three sentences would appear in *The Alcoholics*, a short novel published 21 years later. ('Take a tour of hell,' recommended *New Republic*.) Harlow quivered, shuddered, pulsed, pulsed and throbbed, throbbed and shook and twisted, rolled and rocked, became hot, flushed, shivered with satisfaction, with gratification, felt the slashing acute zest of sensuality, its expanding ecstasy, its electric delight, the happiness, the joy, O, O, O, O! and as Eliot toiled excitedly towards his own climax he became aware of how their sexual energy had spread to affect the entire room, the walls rippling like jelly, the books starting to dance on the shelving, the books so excited that some of them jumped away from their associates and flew to the floor, where a striped rug moved as if a snake was beneath it, and the framed watercolor of 'Sunset Over the Golden Gate Bridge' skipped from its brass hook and flew to the floor, where it shattered, the glass fragments, infected by the general mood, enjoying a brief St Vitus' dance, until, having both enjoyed orgasm, the two lovers lay still, a little sweaty, breathing heavily, fatigued by the effort they'd put into their performance, coinciding with the jittery broken glass calming down and finally becoming still.

In time he finally separated from Harlow – a peculiar suction had joined their gleaming bellies and there was a strange squelching popping burst of sound as they came apart.

'Quake,' Harlow said, raising herself up on her elbows and surveying the damage. She lit a cigarette.

'I guess so.'

Eliot was a little disappointed to discover that the wreckage in the room was the consequence of subterranean activity and not of his pleasuring of a screen goddess. The shock was, in fact, a trifling local spasm of the Puente Hills

Thrust, which would not be identified by geologists for another 67 years.

Naked, Eliot went to the window.

Outside all the lights were out. The sidewalks were covered in leaves, shaken from the trees. Down the street the sign on the Hotel de Paris had lost its moorings and hung at a crazy angle. Neon blood no longer pulsed through its veins. And on the corner the copper beech had crashed down on to the convenience store, breaking the iron gate that cowboys tethered their horses to.

He turned back to the room and faced her. 'Do you know I love you?'

'These things happen. They can't be helped.'

'I dream about you every night. I dream of the day when we can be together, just the two of us. We'll live in a house by the ocean and make babies.'

'I like my milk warm, with foam on it,' she whispered. And then she said: 'Oh my Lord!'

Hurriedly she dragged on her clothes. She arranged the dead fox around her shoulders. 'My Cabriolet!' she wailed.

'Honey – it's only a car!'

'It's not the car,' she sobbed. 'It's what I left there!'

She borrowed his flashlight. At the door she turned and stared at him.

'I'll be back!'


She returned some three minutes later, carrying a brown package tied with string.

'This is all mine. This is the most precious, darling thing – so you take damned good care of it, Mr Eliot Blunt!' Her eyes were saucy yet commanding.

She laid it on a table which the props department had put

there for this moment.

'What is it?'

Her face filled with pride, with pleasure, with all the serenity of the accomplished artist. 'It's my novel.'

'Your novel!' Now it was Eliot's turn for the eyes to enlarge and become a little globular. His heart began knocking at the gate of his ribs. The porter was in no hurry to open it.

'I didn't know you wrote fiction!'

Harlow chuckled. 'My big secret.' But then her face became melancholy. 'Paul told me this was a mistake. He said the public loved me for my acting. He wouldn't even read it. He said nobody can be an actress *and* a novelist. It's one or the other. He said M-G-M wouldn't allow it.'

'Outrageous.'

'I wasn't happy. It broke my heart. I said some awful things. Then I went to mother's. And he stayed home and shot himself!'

'You poor baby!'

So that was it. When she'd phoned him that morning and talked about regretting what she'd written she meant her novel! Until this point Eliot wondered if maybe she'd shot her husband then faked his suicide note and that was the writing she'd been referring to. Not that it would really have made any difference. Blondes can get away with murder, everyone knew that. You wouldn't hold a spot of horseplay with a pistol against a fresh blonde widow.

He hugged her. He understood. He wouldn't have blamed her if she *had* been a killer. Rejection is a terrible thing for a writer. It can result in murderous impulses. Eliot had his own mental hit-list of people in the publishing and film industry.

She hugged him back.

Half an hour later the Puente Hills Thrust released an aftershock that again rattled cutlery drawers, upended tall vases, brought down a power line which exploded in a yellow ball, and caused a water mains to burst so that thick grey water squirted fiercely from the hot steaming asphalt in a terrific pulsing jet tall as a Monterey cypress.

'I needed that,' Harlow whispered, as the shaken pages of fallen books settled like slow winter snow flecked with soot. Her eyes were drowsy and a sluggish smile stretched her dimple.

Eliot nodded. 'Later we should go for a ride. There's a restaurant I know. It's one of the best restaurants in the universe.'

'Bung-o,' Harlow said. She was almost asleep.

'You can get roast young sucking pig there. Scotch eggs. Spanish red. The works.'

Harlow didn't reply. She was asleep, breathing in slow heavy rhythms that sounded like soft delicate potent thinly wired machinery working to keep an angel aloft.

# 10

A TELEPHONE RANG and rang. Eliot pulled the pillow over his head and held it tight with both hands. Finally the faraway bells stopped.

This kept happening. It happened over many hours, maybe for days. Eliot felt brain-fogged, tired, somnolent, languid, inert, satiated. Harlow was there and then she was not there. *She look'd at me as she did love, and made sweet moan...* He heard her in the john. A sweet short trumpet solo. The soft gentle percussion of six brief small-volume globular impacts upon a tranquil pond. Then, after a roar of liquid applause, she returned and they began again. They did plenty. They shuddered, spasmed, cried out, slept, woke. He knocked up snacks in the dinette and brought them back to bed. They ate, they smoked cigarettes, they talked, drank, began again...

Harlow whispered sweetly of her enthusiasm for series fiction. 'Romain Rolland, he's so swell. Of course I guess you know he won the Nobel Prize for the lofty idealism of his literary production and the sympathy and love of truth with which he described different types of human beings.'

And another time: 'I'm just *wild* for all ten volumes of *Jean-Christophe*. Heck, it's even better than *The Forsyte Saga*.'

And, later, 'You must know *Kristin Lavransdatter*. Wow!'

And, finally, 'Do you know *Jacob's Room*?'

'Know it, sugar babe? Why, I'm adapting it for the big screen!'

'Jeepers creepers! That's swell!'

But there was a misunderstanding. She had not said *Jacob's Room* but Jakob Wassermann. Author of her favourite novel of all: *The World's Illusion*.

Eliot hadn't read it.

He lost all sense of time, of night and day. What that pale orb which watched them through the drawn curtains might be – whether the shining pockmarked moon or the golden velvet-misted Californian sun – he knew not. More lines from Keats billowed up and drifted in slow motion across the room while Ernest Dowson whispered dreamily from just beyond the bed's edge.

They are not long, the days of wine and roses. Eliot sank into sleep again. And then the time came when he surfaced and she was not there and she was not in the john. She'd gone. He wondered if he had the memory of her kissing him, of whispering endearments and promises. Or was this just a dream?

He left the bed and made his way in all his naked manly splendor across the dim, curtained bedroom.

Eliot looked in the bathroom mirror at the white mask with the dark hollow eyes and the cheeks which had the pallor of a corpse.

It was time to get rid of that souvenir of Venice. He'd only kept it in case he ever needed to rob a bank.

When he'd emptied his bladder he carried out a short private investigation into the space-time continuum. He established it was Friday afternoon, just gone four. There was a note propped against a prop.

*Read it dearest dear and tell me what you think. This story came to me in a dream. I wrote it down exactly as I remembered it. Every gosh darned word!*

*Thanks my darling, lovely Eliot for EVERYTHING (big wink!)*

*J xx*

Eliot took a shower and dressed. He lit a cigarette. Then he made himself a whiskey sour and cut the string around the package. He removed the crisp brown paper and stared at the neat assemblage of typed foolscap pages. Bashed out on an Underwood 5, by the look of the font. He gazed at the title page. *Today is Tonight*. And underneath: *by Jean Harlow*.

An electric thrill ran through him. What a title! What did it mean? The ambiguity was awesome. Titles usually spelt it out. *Mrs Dalloway* was about Mr Dalloway's wife. *Anna Karenina* was about a crazy Russian dame. *War and Peace* was about battles and stuff. *An American Tragedy* was about greed and murder. But what did 'today is tonight' *mean*? How could today possibly be tonight? It just wasn't possible. The day ended and the night began.

Eliot sensed he was in the presence of genius. The title alone gave him the feeling that he was entering a world where nothing was stable and fixed. To achieve that with just three words – my God! Even Shakespeare would have been envious!

He lifted away the title sheet and began reading the first page, the first chapter…

Beginnings are never easy.

There is the direct approach. For example:

*I am a sick man…*

And

*In the late summer of that year we lived in a house in a village that looked across the river and the plain to the mountains.*

And

*It is imperative that now at once, while these stupendous events are still clear in my mind, I should set them down with that exactness of detail which time may blur.*

And

*At the little town of Vevey, in Switzerland, there is a particularly comfortable hotel.*

And

*It was just after supper.*

And

*Kennedy is a country doctor, and lives in Colebrook, on the shore of Eastbay.*

But there is also the more elusive, oblique mysterious touch of one who has truly mastered – mistressed! – their craft. *Today is Tonight* begins with five simple words.

*Something is tickling my nose.*

Dazzling.

Whose nose is this? Is there a debt – the languid oblique confident acknowledgement of greatness which has gone before – to Nikolai Gogol?

Engagement is instantaneous.

*Something* – but what *is* this mysterious source of the light, playful agitation of a nose?

But is it light, is it really playful? Or is it, perhaps, something sinister, something monstrous?

Transfixed, overwhelmed, the reader's eye moves on.

*Something yellow.*

Yellow!

A far from innocent color. Horror continues to vibrate and shimmer at the edge of possibility. It casts the faint shadow of something leprous, or jaundiced and cowardly, and unimaginably vile. Had darling Jean been reading Charlotte Perkins Gilman?

And then – the dreadful spectre vanishes in a cheerful sunlit instant, dispersed by an author fully in control of her materials – *It must be the sheet--*

The tense is that of the present and the point of view is that of the first-person. The reader is there, living each moment as it happens. Excitingly, by the end of that third sentence, the author shows her disdain for periods. She prefers, as Laurence Sterne did, the dash. A typographical gesture indicating that the human mind never quietly closes down a thought but rather rushes off to another one, like a lurcher in a field of rabbits.

Those three opening sentences take the reader into a human mind. But whose?

Dizzyingly, the second paragraph moves abruptly into the third person.

*She raised a pale brown hand, which felt strangely ownerless, and flicked away the corner of the yellow sheet which had fluttered across her face. It was a satin sheet, the color of a pale young begonia bud.*

Two things may be noted about this paragraph, Eliot thought. The first is the way in which the modern condition of alienation and the fracturing of the self are invoked by that *strangely ownerless* hand. Here is a woman who is no longer at home with her own body. It is as if it no longer entirely belongs to her. And secondly, note the repetition of the word 'pale'. A pale hand, a pale bud. There is color, yes – but it has a bloodless, withdrawn quality. And as an adjective it seems stale, dead, second-hand. Eliot wondered if Harlow had been reading Hugo von Hofmannsthal. Surely a sophisticated reader like Harlow, who had an intimate knowledge of modern European literature as approved by no less an authority than the Nobel Committee itself, knew *Ein Brief*.

This suspicion grew as Eliot lit another cigarette, refilled his glass, and read more.

At first Harlow used a collage technique, alternating the

first and third persons as if the vertiginous perspectives of classic modernism were second nature to her. And, like many of the classic modernist writers, she withheld crucial information. Who was this 'she'? This enigmatic un-named woman's streams of consciousness were of the same magnitude as those of Molly Bloom: nudity, the male gaze, sun tan oil, the cost of nightwear, orchids...

And then back to the third person. A morning breeze from Long Island Sound blows into this bedroom. It is September, 9.15am. The chapter ends with another elongated dash – a stiff Corporal-Trim-style flourish, a breaking-off, an intimation, possibly, of intriguing horizontal aspects to the tale that follows.

The first chapter was barely a page of typescript. Eliot moved on impatiently through the pile. Chapter Two introduces Peter Lansdowne, a successful stockbroker, sitting on a swivel chair in his New York office. It is 10.26am and we learn that he is waiting for four more minutes to elapse. The door leading to the outer office catches his attention. He stares at the strange lettering. ENWODSNAL DNA SDLONYER. Below these words is a fourth: SREKORB. But when the door swings inward the meaning becomes plain. These are words seen from the rear!

Harlow's defamiliarizing techniques were stunning, Eliot thought. The sense of strangeness expands as Lansdowne asks his secretary what day it is and then what year. She looks at him with drawn eyebrows and gives him the information he requires. 21 September 1929.

Has Lansdowne lost his mind?

As the reader plunges into a void of mystery the focus shifts. Suddenly all becomes clear. This is a moving tale of romance in which a loving husband drops even an important business meeting in order to telephone his wife Judy at 10.30am. Which he proceeds to do. For at this moment they will have been married for exactly four years.

And Judy is the woman in the first chapter!

Husband and wife exchange wry, tender greetings. They are very deeply in love – but they are also united by their sense of humour. They don't say 'twenty-first' but in a comic acknowledgement of the vernacular of the Eastern seaboard, 'twenty-foist'.

What wags!

We learn a little more about Judy. She is a strange, sensual woman. We learn that she enjoys tearing up orchids and crushing the petals into her skin. *It gives me a funny feeling*, she divulges. We learn that Peter and Judy are hosting a party for friends at their home this coming evening.

Chapter Three. Eliot lit another cigarette. Now he was back in bed with Judy: *the purple velvet petals of the orchids which fluttered against her bare shoulders made her blood tingle as though Peter himself were still caressing her.*

She recalls her wedding day. Eliot learned that the best man, Bill Reynolds, her husband's business partner – SDLONYER! – has always been in love with her. Judy knew it but in the end chose Peter. But it's okay because the three of them are still the best of pals.

And now back to the present. Harlow tells of a party with Judy and Peter's wild, wild friends. Vance Stephens – a single man and a lecherous drunk. Sally Everett – 26, a widow and a lecherous drunk. Allen and Ethel Boettiger. Bill Reynolds. Hank and Wilma Bestor. Hester and George Van Buren. Edward Monteith and his unnamed wife. The whiskey sours and the cocktails flow. New Orleans Fizz. Lots of Tom and Jerry. Peter gives Judy two anniversary presents. The first is a dachshund. *Judy immediately liked his grave mien and steady eyes, which might have been those of a wise old philosopher.* The second is three bracelets of platinum, diamonds and emeralds. Lecherous Sally attempts to seduce Peter: *She twisted her body to one side to show, casually, an entertaining expanse of spinal torso.* But Peter is immune to its splendour. Judy, who is watching, leads him outside. There, on the beach, they make passionate love in the moonlight. While this is going on Sally flirts with Bill. But Bill is indifferent to her charms.

Chapter Eight. The next morning. Judy is once again in bed. She has a slight headache but feels warm and happy. Downstairs she finds Peter, Bill, Hank, and Sally at the breakfast table, arguing over sections of the morning paper. As Judy is staring at her ham and eggs enter Wilma, Allen, Ethel, Peggy, George, Hestor and the Monteiths. Then Vance appears, holding the slipper that Judy left behind on the beach. He says there is clear evidence of 'monkey business' on the sand last night. Judy cheerily admits that she and Peter had sex there. Every woman in the room envied her, while the men tried *to visualize Peter's mental retrospections.*

And on this edgy, electric sexy note the chapter ends. *Sex* — that seemed to be constantly on the author's mind — along with beds and daydreams. Eliot smiled wistfully and refilled his glass.

Next he turned the unread pile upside down. He quickly established that there were forty chapters in all. He flipped the manuscript over again, which made him think of Mildred. Eliot, trembling a little, began reading Chapter Nine.

Peter and four of the guests go riding. Judy stays behind. She says she's in no condition to be bounced around in the saddle. Wilma, Hank, Bill and Sally join Peter. Off they gallop. Ninety minutes of riding, with badinage. And then it happens. Just as Peter is about to jump a fence a rabbit shoots out of a thicket, frightening his horse. Its forelegs hit the top rail and Peter is thrown off. The horse lands, striking Peter in the head with a hoof.

Chapter Ten. Peter is brought home, unconscious. Judy sees them approaching and realises something awful has happened. *An icicle of fear stabbed through her head.* They lay Peter on the marital bed. Dr Monteith diagnoses a fractured skull. He says there is no immediate danger. As a student of language and meaning Judy cleverly realises this means that there might be danger in the future. Peter is not yet out of the woods! *The dagger of ice resting in her brain seemed to melt, the drops flowed in and around every little nook and cranny of her consciousness, and the drops of melted ice were more bitterly freezing than the icicle itself had been.*

Roll over Virginia Woolf, Eliot thought. Harlow was much better at names – at thoughts and emotions and dialogue, too. And her poetic style was out of this world!

He had another drink and smoked another cigarette.

Dr Monteith calls in an expert, Dr Frederick Gerhardt who, assisted by two nurses, will operate on Peter in the house, since it is too dangerous to move him.

Judy has a meltdown and is sedated and put to bed. A week passes. It is too early to determine whether or not the operation has succeeded. But then the day comes when she is taken upstairs to learn the terrible truth. Peter will live but he's lost his sight!

Something inside Judy seems to explode. She has to fight hard against a blackness which wants to swallow her. The room begins to whirl round and round.

Judy experiences that same horror and void which the great modernists sought to articulate. Language seems to crumble and lose all meaning. *Words came to her lips, which meant nothing to her. They were just words.*

Eliot had to pause and refill his glass. He lit another cigarette. He was trembling. He felt like he'd been living in the room across the hall from a pudgy, bald fellow who said he worked in the entertainment industry. And one day the guy had knocked on his door and handed him a bunch of paper and said: 'Wondered if you wouldn't mind taking a look at this, buddy. I'd value your opinion.' 'Sure thing, buster. Be happy to.' And then taking it indoors and looking at it under the light of a candle you saw that the first page was headed: *The Tragedie of Hamlet, Prince of Denmarke.*

Yes, Harlow was *that* damned good. And like the bald bard she was both an actor *and* a writer. And like her predecessor she was at home with antidiplosis, catachresis, epistrophe, hypophora, paronomasia, stichomythia and zeugma.

And, most of all, human suffering.

*Peter – blind!*

Judy is quick to point out to her husband the advantages of his new condition. He will be spared ever again having to look at any of *the little tired mean things* in the world that others are forced to witness! As for the rest – from now on she's going to be a pair of spectacles for him, wrapping everything in pink ribbon! Heck, there's no reason to be downhearted! She clings to his arm. 'Why, Peter, the happiest times you've had were when you couldn't see because there wasn't any light in the room!' (They have sex in the dark, it seems.)

And Peter tells her that it's okay. He really doesn't mind at all about losing his sight.

*

Eliot refreshed his glass and sent some Benzedrine on a trip to his guts.

He read Chapter Eleven in just a couple of minutes. It was very short. Judy is in bed again – sleeping alone. Peter is in the next room, attended by a nurse. And Judy recalls the words of Dr Gerhardt, who recommended visiting the great eye specialist Brenner at Johns Hopkins.

Chapter Twelve: Bill phones Judy four times a day. Judy encourages Peter to return to the master bedroom.

Chapter Thirteen: Judy and Peter drive to the Pennsylvania Station to take the train to Baltimore. Meanwhile the Wall Street crash begins.

Chapter Fourteen: Dr Brenner examines Peter and concludes his blindness is permanent. They return distraught to New York. The Wall Street crash worsens.

Chapter Fifteen: The couple return to their lovely Elizabethan house in Westchester. Judy receives an urgent call from Bill. He asks her to come into the office tomorrow. When she does she learns that the business has gone bust. Bill and Peter are bankrupt.

Eliot yawned. He felt emotionally drained. Harlow's title still baffled him but he'd read more of the manuscript tomorrow, Saturday.

He went to bed. Before putting out the light he took three teaspoons of chloral and two Nembutals. Chloral was a delicious word but Nembutal was sweeter.

That night he dreamed he was staying at 8221 Sunset Boulevard. He was in the Chateau bar, which was empty apart from the barman. The man stood there motionless in a plum-colored velvet smoking jacket with a bow tie and a high collar. 'A little slow tonight, isn't it?' Eliot remarked, adding:

'Give me a bottle of bourbon, a glass and some ice.' 'Certainly, sir,' the man replied. He took down a bottle of Jack Daniel's and laid it on the bar. Eliot grinned wolfishly, rolled his eyes maniacally and winked knowingly. 'You set 'em up and I'll knock 'em back, one by one.' Then, mysteriously, the bottle was empty, the ice was gone, and he was upstairs, gliding along a corridor with a thick, soft, blood-red carpet. Eliot was slightly on fire but the flames didn't seem to hurt. They flickered along the undersides of his arms and around his thighs. He was looking for his room but he wasn't sure which floor he was on. There were so many doors, not all of them numbered. The place had more doors than the fun house at Ocean Park pier.

At last he came to his room. He unlocked the door and went in. To his surprise the youngest of Irving Thalberg's three secretaries was there, in the final stages of getting undressed. The door to the bathroom opened and out stepped Millard Coleman in a bath robe. 'What in hell are you doing here?' he shouted.

'Sorry – wrong room,' Eliot said. 'I was looking for 96.' He knew now he was in 69.

'But there is no room 96 at the Chateau,' Coleman said, frowning.

And then the bedroom was full of yellow light and the birds were singing and there were traffic noises in the street.

It was the start of another L.A. day.

# 11

SATURDAY.

Eliot shaved and showered. He ate ham and eggs washed down with two black coffees and fourteen teaspoons of sugar. Then he sat down again with Harlow's manuscript. He had some serious reading ahead of him. He lit a cigarette, lined up some Bix Beiderbecke for the victrola, and set to work to the sound of 'Royal Garden Blues'.

The next ten chapters seemed to fly by. Peter becomes depressed and searches for his revolver, to kill himself. Judy stops him. She holds him tight. They still have each other. The bankrupt Lansdownes have to leave their fabulous house and move to an apartment on East 63rd Street. Heart-breakingly, the Duesenberg and the Ford Station Wagons have to be sold, along with the jewellery that Peter gives Judy in Chapter Five and his beloved copy of the portrait of Pope Innocent X by Velazquez. Bill hungers for Judy but is restrained by decency. Peter starts to get ratty. Judy agrees to participate in a charity event as Lady Godiva. Her performance arouses considerable interest. Afterwards she receives a letter from Herbert Wolfson, theatrical agent. *Wolfson*! Had Harlow chosen this name having heard of Eliot's own Woolf treatments, he wondered?

The theatrical agent invites Judy to his office. He has a proposition. As she waits to see him, Judy stares at the autographed celebrity photographs on the wall. She is surprised to see that the autographs are white! She never knew that white ink existed.

A nice touch, that, Eliot thought. Because there is something deeply subversive about white ink. It turns language inside out! Can you imagine Shakespeare's sonnets written in white ink? White on white is *nothing* – nothing at all. Eliot suddenly had an idea for a novel about a great writer whose genius goes unrecognised because everything he writes is written in white ink. No one can read a word! The novelist doesn't publish a single book. When he dies, a very old man, he leaves behind the manuscripts of nine of the greatest novels ever written. But, sorting out his effects after his death, the novelist's widow sees only a collection of scrap paper. She uses the manuscripts to write shopping lists and to light fires in winter.

White ink also reminds the reader of Peter. His is a black world, in which print – black text – is lost in the greater absence of light and contrast.

The layers of meaning in Harlow's novel were out of this world. Truly she was in the same sphere as that high lustrous one where the immortals cruise like slow glorious comets across a firmament of purple light infused with an Elysian glow.

Twelve noon. Time for a beer. Eliot felt he had shown extraordinary restraint in keeping to coffee for so long.

He lit another cigarette and stared thoughtfully at the corner where the spider sometimes crouched. On the far side of the room Bix tapped out 'In a Mist'. Eliot finished his second beer. Now Harlow's story was really starting to speed up. Lunch could wait.

*Lunch could wait!* That thought gave him the spark for another book. Or at least a movie treatment. As a title it was electrifying, though the tense would need adjusting. *Lunch Can Wait*. A screwball comedy. Suggestive – but quintessentially clean, wholesome family fare.

But this idea would itself have to wait. Harlow's tale drew

all his attention. Eliot picked up the typed sheet and read on.

The agent makes Judy an offer. He wants her to do her nude Lady Godiva act at the Club Heron for 250 bucks a week. Judy merrily retorts that what he's suggesting seems to involve a horse and her wearing little more than a surcingle. Eliot, who was not an equestrian, had to go to the dictionary to look that word up. He felt humbled that Harlow's vocabulary was greater than his own. She sure as jiminy was a gal and a half.

Judy says yes. But there's a problem where Peter is concerned. The hours of employment are from 7pm until late. How can she conceal her new occupation from her husband?

This is where Harlow's genius for plotting shines. She realises that a blind person can't possibly tell the difference between day and night! All Judy has to do is re-arrange his schedule without him noticing! It was absurdly easy because *time is a flirtatious mistress*. She brings him his breakfast at dusk and says she's going out for the day to help with charity work. Easy-peasy! And off she goes. And so Chapter Twenty-Six ends: *His today was her tonight. Today is tonight.*

Eliot felt very strongly every novel should explain its title, preferably by embedding it directly in the text, with spotlights and a frame. This Harlow had dazzlingly, deliciously, and daringly done.

The next chapter. Judy goes off to perform nude at the Club Heron. But – clever Judy! – she protects her modesty by applying lanolin cold cream a quarter of an inch thick around her lower regions. A lesser woman, greasy as this, might slide off her horse. Not Judy. But horror! In a moment of Dickensian coincidence Bill Reynolds turns up on her first night and recognises her by – surprise plot twist! – the anklet of small pearls on her left ankle. Bill knows that Judy *never* takes off that anklet. Afterwards Bill takes her back to his place. He waits to hear her explanation. Judy bursts into tears. *The moment her tears flowed freely, Judy felt better. That is what tears are for.*

Bill says he'll give her 250 dollars to spare her from having to appear naked as a living. She says she knows he doesn't have that kind of money. But she'd be grateful to use his pad to crash out in after the show and before it's time to go home and pretend it's night.

Agreed.

Arriving back home Judy finds her husband in an ebullient mood. In her absence Peter has found some cord in a drawer and rigged it up to guide him across the room. He says he realises he can develop this scheme to provide him with an efficient way of finding his way around their apartment while she's out doing her charity work.

The marital mood is bubbly. Judy reflects that the ease with which she talks about gender and psychology shows that she would find it very easy to write a book about philosophy. But this leads on to the recognition that philosophy is grounded in language, which imposes limitations on understanding. *All sentences beginning with the words 'All sentences' are silly. Maybe all sentences themselves are silly.*

Eliot was stunned. Son of a bitch! Had Wittgenstein travelled to Hollywoodland? Eliot felt distinctly peeved. Sometimes it's nice to know that only *you* know about a cult writer. A good cult writer is a secret to be nursed, not shared. Something happens when a writer on the edge goes mainstream. Some strange vulgarisation takes place. Suddenly the text becomes a cheap commodity, appropriated, part of the cultural furniture. It loses its freshness, its uniqueness. It becomes commonplace.

But there was no getting away from it. Harlow knew her *Tractatus Logico-Philosophicus*.

Bix did 'Futuristic Rhythm' and Eliot paused to crack open a bag of Bull Durham tobacco. He spread it on a paper and rolled another number. The match crackled and he inhaled. He matched it with another beer. He returned to the text.

Horror! Peter, having cleverly established a network of cords to feel his way around, works up the confidence to leave the apartment. He befriends an Irish taxi driver, who reveals that day is night and night is day! Peter's new friend goes with him back to the apartment. He reports that a beautiful copper-haired woman has arrived outside the building, with a male companion.

More horror! Peter now knows that Judy has been two-timing him. He greets her coldly. She worries he's found out. But how can he have done? Judy reflects on the subjectivity of American time. Eastern Standard Time. Central Standard Time. Mountain Standard Time. Pacific Standard Time. So many variable times! And at this moment the reader surely remembers that moment when Judy held her husband tight, just after saving him from shooting himself. *Silence. The tall grandfather's clock sent its melancholy ticktack, ticktack, ticktack out of its shadowy corner. Into the racked consciousness that Judy vaguely knew to be her own came the incoherent memory that the minute hand of the clock needed fixing.* A reflection which deliberately plays upon that classic question: *Pray, my dear, have you not forgot to wind up the clock?*

Peter's suspicions grow. He tells his wife to stop doing her charity work. The tension rises. Judy pours herself a glass of Scotch. She drinks it slowly. She feels the raw liquor sting her throat. *It helped to give her a feeling of reality.*

Eliot felt the same. Harlow's words had given him a serious thirst. He went to the kitchenette and returned with a bottle of hootch. He rolled another cigarette. He drank. The sky outside was brilliant and clear. A scrap of moon hung there like a piece of flaked-off skin. Eliot heard wheels outside. He heard wheels inside. They had rubber tyres and made a slight hiss.

He read on.

Peter Lansdowne starts to visit nightclubs with his friendly Irish taxi driver. He finds work on a newspaper writing a column about night club life. And then – roll of drums – at the close of Chapter Thirty-Four he sets out for the Heron Club.

Eliot could see there weren't many sheets left in the pile. The End was near.

Chapter Thirty-Five. Judy arrives at Bill's apartment, as she always does after a show. Her mind is as exposed as her body has recently been. *I've got to have a drink. I wonder if I'm getting to be a real drunkard? No. I'm drinking only because I have to have something to keep me going.*

Quite. Eliot raised his glass to that infinitely wise per-ception. Good ol' Jean! A shmart gal. Triffic writer.

Then Bill arrives. He sees she's hitting the hard stuff. He asks if she's going to leave her husband.

Oh. My. God.

Eliot was astonished.

Earlier on in the novel Harlow had slipped in an allusion to Shakespeare's *Julius Caesar*. But now – now she really let loose. Her literary ambition was colossal. She let rip.

'Never – never – never – never – never,' Judy replies.

*'You can't keep this up!' he remonstrated.*

Poor Bill. He is oblivious to the words which have tumbled

from Judy's sweet red lips. The poor sap has never seen *King Lear*, let alone read it.

No matter.

Judy promptly has sex with Bill.

But the next night when she turns up at Bill's with Bill, Peter is there! The truth comes out. Judy loves both of them! She pours out her heart, then rushes away.

The two men are left to talk about the situation. Peter puts his arm around Bill and asks what happened to the bottle of Scotch...

*Gockle o'scorch.*

A thick sea fog blew in across the bay. Out there in the murk a foghorn blasted its warnings like some great bellowing beast in agony. Eliot made his way past the flamboyant simile and continued along a deserted quayside. He slipped up the gangway and onto the great ship. Opening a hatch he descended several flights of iron stairs to the thumping heart of the vessel. There at the end of the corridor he saw her. Harlow. She was clothed only in transparent scarves and she was doing a strange wild dance, swaying, her arms making writhing, snaking movements. She didn't seem to see him. The scarves rose up, exposing her magnificent flanks, her firm full breasts, the rich clump of platinum grass at the fork of her body.

She saw Eliot and laughed. Her laughter tumbled along the corridor towards him. It repeated itself as echoes which grew smaller and smaller. At the same time Harlow seemed to shrink, becoming a miniature of herself, reduced to no more than a dime, then a single tiny dot of whiteness.

His attention was wrenched away by a wild animal which burst blackly and blurrily from a side panel. It snapped at his right hand. Its teeth savagely sank through skin and muscle.

With a grunt of pain and shock Eliot woke to find his smouldering cigarette had burned itself down to his fingers.

He swore and dropped it into the overflowing ashtray, then ran to put his fingers under the cold tap. Nothing happened to ease the pain so he tried turning the tap on. That was better. He saw that it was 5pm. He needed to sober up before the next round of liquor. Plus he felt hungry. Eliot drank two black coffees with plenty of sugar. He fixed himself some 1932 food. The details could wait for the second draft. Whatever it was he ate it sure tasted good. It supplied the nutrition he needed to carry him on to the end of Harlow's manuscript.

He put the dishes in the sink and returned to the table where the manuscript lay in two neat piles. The novel was almost over now.

Judy goes back to see the two men in her life. She says she's realised she can't have both – not sexually. (Why not? thought Eliot.) So she's made her choice. Judy asks Bill to leave the room while she talks to her husband. It sounds like Peter is toast. But then – amazing plot twist! – the reader learns that she's chosen to stay with her husband. Peter tells her everything will be okay from now on. *I've got a job. I'm doing newspaper work. I write a daily column 'Broadway By A Blind Man'. Judy, it's – it's swell.'*

Yes, indeedy. Who wouldn't want to read a blind man's regular accounts of the latest shows?

Judy talks of them having a baby.

Bill goes home. He solemnly accepts that Judy's made her choice. The three of them remain the best of friends. Judy's night of sex with Bill casts no shadow over this chummy chuckling trio's cheery chatter or chortles.

THE END

Eliot pushed the chair back.

He felt emotionally, physically and intellectually drained. He'd never read anything quite like this manuscript before. It was almost indescribable.

He couldn't wait to tell Harlow his reaction.

But first he needed a nap. The booze and the book had wiped him out. He went back to the bedroom, crawled on top of his bed, and dozed.

# 12

FOR A WHILE ALL was well and then he felt a terrible cramp in both legs. He was unable to move. A hatch in the floor opened and a seal poked its head out. The seal watched him for a while, then slipped back into the floor at the sound of the elevator. The cage went clickety-click as it approached. Eliot heard the door slide open with a metallic squeal. Someone walked down the corridor with a slow, heavy footstep. They approached his door. It was intensely cinematic.

A fist smashed against the panelling, making the door shudder. The fist continued to hit the door. It seemed to match exactly the loud knocking of Eliot's swollen, pain-filled heart.

And then a drill started up. Someone was drilling into his front door. It was high, screeching noise which was painful to hear. The needle of sound seemed to melt into something else. A bell. The tinny protracted shrill spurt of his front door bell.

Eliot woke, soaked in sweat.

There was someone at his front door, ringing the bell.

Groaning, he rolled out of bed and tottered off to see who it was.


The woman who stood there wore a white trench coat which went down to her shins.

'I've missed you,' she said.

'Mildred!'

She pushed him gently backwards into the room. In her left fist she held a bottle. She grinned. 'Celebration time, bright eyes.'

'Where have you been? Why haven't you called? I saw you at Bern's funeral! You ran away from me!'

'I had to leave town. I wasn't at no funeral, honey. Maybe it was my twin sister.'

'You have a twin sister!'

'Sure. Margaret. Identical to me in most ways. Except not so nice.'

'But – '

Mildred had found her way to the kitchen. She was fiddling with the cork. There was a sudden crack like a shot had been fired. Eliot's body jerked in shock. The cork flew up, hit the ceiling, and then bounced around the floor a few times.

'This here is very special booze,' Mildred said. She held up two tumblers of the bubbling liquid. It was the color of urine. 'All the way from Paree, France.'

She held out a glass. 'Here's to it!'

Eliot sniffed it. The fluid had a bitter aroma. He decided to let Mildred drink hers first, just to be careful. He'd read a lot of crime novels. He knew you had to be careful with dames like Mildred. They knew their arsenic from their edea.

She upended and imbibed, so he did too. A new warmth flooded his tired flesh. Soon the bottle was empty.

'Hey, your coat!'

Mildred grinned. 'I was saving it for now.' She slipped the coat off and let it fall to the floor.

'Jeepers!'

Mildred smirked. 'I thought you'd like it.'

Eliot trembled. 'You're a knockout!'

Beneath the coat she was wearing a pair of black leather boots that ran up beyond her knees. They enclosed a pair of black stockings and a suspender belt. That was pretty much it. In fact that was totally it.

Eliot felt a familiar pressure in his pants.

No, he thought. This would be quite wrong. He was Harlow's, now. He must not betray her. Besides, this bitch had fiddled with his books and stolen several of his Woolfs – including the signed one.

'Hey! You took my copy of *The Waves*!'

Mildred peeled away his clothes and began to fondle him. 'We'll talk about that later,' she grunted.

'No, this isn't right!'

But he did not push her away. Heck, Harlow would never know. And he was but a man – a poor forked animal, chained to a preposterous and unruly appendage. It stretched itself in its cage, tiger-like, hungry for meat.

Mildred kneeled and applied her tongue. Then she took him by the hand and led him to the bed. Almost at once they were connected and writhing.

Afterwards they lay awhile chatting. She apologised for the Woolf appropriation. He'd get them back, promise. Then she told him all about her twin, Margaret, and the problems it caused. She explained about her sudden trip to Ohio to see her poor sick momma. She'd been so busy looking after her there just hadn't been the chance to tell Eliot what was going on. She hoped he'd forgive her.

He said he did.

'You're so damn sweet!' There were tears in her eyes. They repeated their sweaty, noisy performance. After that they dressed and Mildred went off to make coffee.

'I should do that, sweetest plum.'

'No, really. This is woman's work. How many sugars?'

'Seven.'

'Coming right up, mister!'

He gulped the hot liquid down. He felt a great hunger for a steak and fries, slathered in sauce, with a heap of half-incinerated onion.

And then something strange occurred. Eliot felt his chest contract. The room developed a mild spin.

'Quake,' he said – though it came out as 'quirk'.

Mildred stared at him. It was a cold, hard stare. It seemed to lose focus. In the mist he could see a red curve which looked like a smile.

'Feeling... ' How did Eliot feel? Ropy. Fatigued. Loose. Slack. Weak.

He staggered forwards. The floor moved, trying to tip him over.

'Cough,' he said. 'Cough.'

He was trying to say coffee but he couldn't manage the entire word. Mildred looked at him pityingly. 'Correct, bright eyes. I doped your coffee.'

'Whirr?'

'Because I was paid to, sugar. I'm here to collect. Do you really think I like you, you dumb sap? Well in a way I do. You're cute under the blanket. But frankly I'd never have bothered if Benjamin Franklin hadn't come my way. Regard the fun as a bonus. I could have dropped you into dreamland with the fizz but I didn't. I thought I'd get myself some top class shuddering first. And boy, is you good. But then you're young, relatively. You still have muscle.'

'Wash... whirr... '

'The fact is buster I'm seventeen years older than you. I'm fifty next February. It's a funny thing about men. You don't have a clue about a lady's age. Or maybe you don't care.' She smirked. 'Maybe you just like your steak well marinated. Honey, you wouldn't be the first.'

'Thash... ' Eliot was on his knees now. The room contained an orchestra which couldn't agree which symphony they were playing. Somebody began pumping cement into his head from a noisy, turning cylinder. Now he was lying face down on the beach. The waves were tickling his toes. It reminded him of a novel he'd once read.

He heard a door slam. It triggered an avalanche of grey rock which came bouncing down the slope, struck him on the brow, and buried him alive.

While Eliot is unconscious – perhaps, shortly, he will have a dream that cries out to be told – there's an opportunity to return to his bookshelf and consider an enigmatic sentence in Chapter Three. This refers to his discovery upon returning home on the Monday of Jean Harlow's phone call that his books had been disturbed. There was mention of a pioneering work of literary analysis which concluded with the observation that *The concluding pages* – and so on. This enigmatic citation cries out for explication. Or does it? For it is surely enough to say that the un-named author's analysis of an un-named novel concerns a text initially regarded, according to this critic, as *a violently romantic work* which required rescuing from its enthusiasts and legitimising as a work of solid organisation and strict authorial control. The novel in question, described as impressing the average reader most of all by *the striking psychological realism of the narrative*, and the daring use of words which other writers flinch from, either using terms of endearment, in a decent disguise, or *asterisked out of recognition*, also required recognition of *the unusual angle* from which the author viewed the text's characters – or as our critic puts it – *creatures*. The texts in question – those of the critic and those of the novelist – are, as would be obvious to any 1932 reader with a knowledge of original fiction of the past decade and the commentary it had accreted –

But the voiceover abruptly terminates in mid-sentence. In silence the camera tracks slowly and teasingly along a shelf of spines. You need to tip your head sideways to read the titles. *Hypersensualism: A Practical Philosophy for Acrobats. Picture-Minded. The Insignificance of Significance. Herbert Strang's Annual, 1920. Journal of a Pointless Life. The Second Murderer. The Naked Man. Tall Women. The Golden Peepshow. The Norfolk Broads. Three Voyages of a Naturalist. The Cock-Eyed Angel. The One-Eyed Undertaker. Oddities. Seven Men Named Caesar. The Ecstasy Department. Advertisement for Death. Phantom Lady. Love of a Lifetime. Dark Circles. All it needs is Elephants.*

The camera, still in motion, tilts in the direction of the sound-stage floor, where Eliot, sprawled and floppy across the threadbare Mexican rug laid upon a parquet floor – is displaying signs of distress. The actor playing Eliot groans loudly, at a volume loud enough for the unseen microphone to pick up, and moves his limbs in a manner regarded by contemporary drama teaching as best expressing pain and confusion. The legs twitch. The arms move as if Eliot was attempting to stay afloat in a lake with the dense, sucking grip of Grimpen mire.

'Oh, oh, oh, oh... '

'Cut!'

Not a bad effort, on the whole, bearing in mind that the script is dreadful. Clark Gable springs up from the floor, gives a cheery wave to the crew, and goes to his dressing room to wash off the dust.

\*

Eliot drove on past the curve that goes down into the Strip as far as Ecks Street, where a joint called The Garden of Eden had just opened. A snowman sat next to him and there was a small polar bear in the rumble seat. The polar bear said: 'I don't like to think of you unconscious, with a dream incubating. You never know where a dream's going. It might turn into *Freaks*, goddamit.' 'She's right,' the snowman said. 'The scripts are often terrible. As for nonsense about enigmatic sentences in Chapter Three. I mean, buddy, *please*. Nobody wants *to and fro* in a movie. They want action. They want A to Zee. They don't want no messing around with time.'

As he pulled up outside the venue Eliot saw that the snowman had melted, leaving a pungent puddle on the seat.

'You know I can't go in there,' the polar bear said, pointing at the roped-off entrance where a crowd of hopefuls were queuing. Two doormen in scarlet Ruritanian uniforms were vetting everyone seeking admission. 'I'll stay here and take a nap,' the bear said, curling up and closing its eyes. 'I'll see you later, buddy.'

'Sure thing.'

As Eliot approached the entrance one of the doormen saw him. 'Right this way, Mr Blunt!'

The waiting crowd stared enviously. This guy was a big shot. A top writer at M-G-M.

Inside the tables had been pushed back to show a movie on the far wall. There must have been a couple of hundred people there, standing with their drinks, watching the flickering black and white scenes go by.

Eliot saw it was a stag movie. A woman was taking a bath when someone knocked at the door. She wrapped a towel round herself and went to see who it was. It was a boy with a telegram. The woman pulled the boy into the room. Her towel fell to the floor, exposing a chubby bottom and a pair of thick thighs.

In the next shot she was peeling off the lad's clothes. The Garden of Eden crowd cheered wildly at the close-up of an engorged penis. There were shouts, catcalls, more cheering. How merry the mood was in there! Now the youth's small ass could be seen rising and falling between the woman's voluptuous thighs. When the copulation was over the woman gestured in exaggerated surprise. Someone was knocking at her door! She pushed the naked youth into a wardrobe, bundling his clothes in after him. She wrapped her towel around herself and answered the door.

It was one of her lovers. The fellow stepped inside the room, holding a bunch of roses. They embraced. The woman let the towel drop and returned to the bed. Her lover peeled off his clothes.

To his horror Eliot saw that the lover was himself. Others in the crowd seemed to notice this too. People started whispering and pointing.

Now he was on the bed, kneeling between the woman's thighs. The camera tracked towards his swaying penis. The crowd cheered and laughed and pointed. Eliot felt his cheeks turning bright red.

But now the woman on the bed wasn't the chubby one who'd fucked the lad. It was Mildred, in her boots and stockings. As she drew Eliot down inside her a close-up of her face displayed a knowing smile. She winked at the camera.

How the Garden of Eden crowd roared!

Eliot turned and fought his way to the exit.

Men poked him the ribs and shrieked 'Attaboy!' Drunk

women clawed at his shirt and planted kisses on his burning face. Some pressed their hands against his crotch. One woman managed to unbuckle his belt and went exploring. An incandescence washed over him as someone took a picture.

Outside, the polar bear had woken up. It was holding the latest edition of *The Illustrated Daily News*. 'This looks bad,' the bear said, pointing its claws. MOVIE WRITER'S SHAME was the front-page headline. Underneath was a picture of a dishevelled-looking Eliot being embraced by a slutty-looking woman whose right hand was burrowed inside his pants. Beside it was a photograph of him naked, on top of Mildred.

'Oh God,' Eliot sobbed.

'We gotta move,' the bear said. 'Fast.'

Eliot sped off. He needed to get the hell out of L.A. But out on Mulholland Drive something went wrong. The polar bear said: 'I think someone shot me.' Eliot glanced and saw that the creature's white pelt had developed a saucer-sized patch of dark blood. The blood began to expand, creeping across the animal's stomach and chest.

A tire on the car suddenly blew. Eliot struggled to keep control as it thump-thump-thumped and slithered across the highway.

It was no good. He couldn't do it. The car flew off the road and began to roll down the hillside. *Thump! Thump! Thump!* It was exquisitely cinematic. As the car rocked and rolled Eliot felt no pain. All he was aware of was the noise. *Thump! Thump! Thump!*

Someone was knocking at his door. Eliot snapped awake. The room was in darkness. What day was it? Why weren't they using the bell? He went to see who it was.

In the yellow light of the corridor he saw that it was

Millard Coleman. The director's face displayed a strange fixed smile. Eliot's heart was a leathery fist that kept socking him with the word *Mary*. Was that what this was all about? Was this what that was all about? Was about that what this was all? About what was that? Was this? The ground in Los Angeles was anything but solid. Heck, as the man said *Wovon man nicht sprechen kann, darüber muss man schweigen.*

Eliot's furred, blue-grey tongue wriggled in the dripping cavern of his mouth. A tongue's life was hot and furtive and wet. Eliot's tongue had secrets. It was astonishing that no one had ever written a novel – not even a short story! – from the perspective of a tongue. But he guessed there wouldn't be a movie in it – only in a story where a tongue was cut out. That Philomela broad, for instance. But maybe that was too brutal. And the stuff about her turning into a tweety bird wouldn't work. Not unless she became an eagle. Then she could rip the guy apart, the guy who'd taken a knife to her. But no – too much blood. Nobody would like it. A shame.

Eliot's tongue had been to some remarkable places. But this was not the time to let it speak of strawberries and cream. Besides, it had settled down now, like a reptile relaxing in a crevice of wet rock.

'Surprised to see me?' Coleman said.

Eliot nodded. From a room down the corridor he could hear 'Three Blind Mice (Rhythmic Theme in Advanced Harmony)', recorded at Pathé Studios on East 53rd Street, New York City, in October 1927.

The jaundiced director accepted Eliot's whispered invitation to step inside, inside, inside. 'A foul place you have here, idiot,' he surely didn't say, say, say. A swell place, Eliot, surely. Eliot was still groggy from sleep and a head which held the residue of strange dreams.

The diminutive film-maker produced some original dialogue.

'I figured we should talk. Away from the studio.'

Eliot nodded. The director's complexion had the roughness and color of cheese rind.

What time was it? Almost midnight. Eliot offered Coleman liquor or coffee. The director joined him in coffee. This time Eliot made damned sure he was the one who made the drink. Coleman's was taken with milk, no sugar. The writer kept to black with seven teaspoonfuls.

Coleman seemed nervous. 'Have a cigarette,' he said. 'They're special. Largardie & Raymond. Egyptian. I get them direct from the manufacturer.' He took one out of a purple packet and threw it across. Eliot put out his hands to catch it. The cigarette passed between them and softly bounced twice across the Mexican stripes.

It was a handsome item, with the body of a small cigar and a faintly aromatic odour. Eliot lit it and inhaled. A rush of something fiery and wild coursed through his chest. It rose through him and seemed to fill the chambers of his head with colors and mists. There was a church there, too, somewhere – an English church, in a green valley, which bell ringers were filling with medleys of overlapping chimes.

Eliot wondered if marijuana formed part of the mix. 'Shoot,' he said.

'I left my revolver in the Packard,' Coleman replied. 'I knew I'd be tempted.'

'Eh?' Eliot chuckled. The cigarette made him feel elated.

'You've been getting fresh with my wife, you son of a bitch,' the director said.

'New lark hair,' Eliot said. 'Lurk whore. This too sigh... ' He was struggling to articulate the right words.

'You lousy punk. Who in hell do you think you are? A two-bit no-good hack writer like you, harassing my Mary!'

'Thass... thass... nut... nut... '

In some poorly lit segment of Eliot's still alert brain he realised the cigarette was doped. What a mug he'd been. He wasn't learning from experience. In future he knew he must never accept a beer offered by a stranger, a coffee presented to him by a woman of loose morals, or the gift of a cigarette of unusual size which smelled slightly perfumed. Even addled Dr Freud would have sniffed out the meaning of that last one.

Eliot stood. He swayed. He felt he was in a scene he'd played before. Maybe this was simply the sixteenth take.

'You stay away from her,' Coleman said. 'You're frightening her with your pestering and your phone calls and hanging around the places she goes to.'

'Nut... nut... ' What a travesty the director's account had become! He needed to explain. He needed to tell dear old Millard the truth of what had occurred. Problem was his feet seemed nailed to the floor and his voicebox had filled with mud.

'This is from both of us,' Coleman said quietly. He approached, jerked back his right arm, and sent it powering forwards. His fist struck Eliot on the jaw and the writer catapulted backwards, hit the floor, and lay still.

# 13

THE POLAR BEAR SAID: 'I did warn you what would happen. But you just wouldn't listen. You men are all the same.'

Eliot took the roadster down Sunset Boulevard. As they passed The Sunset Tower the snowman beside him grinned, poked him in the ribs with its icy elbow, and said: 'What a magnificent erection!'

But talking isn't good for snowmen. The movement of its crystalline lips caused its drooping carrot nose to loosen and drop away like a tooth.

Eliot drove to the edge and threw himself out, just like James Dean would do twenty-three years later in *Rebel Without A Cause*. He watched as the car plunged away into the darkness. It was hard to tell if the white faces of its two occupants expressed terror or indifference. The snowman looked upset but that was probably because he missed his nose. People would think he had syphilis. The polar bear wore a smile of contentment, common in people who know best.

Eliot walked back a few paces, then ran forwards and threw himself into the void. He had correctly calculated his trajectory and landed safely on top of the cross-bar of the H in the Hollywoodland sign. From there he jumped to L and then from W to D. When he reached the N he halted. The next letter was the thirteenth. But there was already someone standing on it. He recognised her. It was Peg. A fellow Brit. He called across to her: 'My snowman didn't melt after all!' But Peg didn't seem to hear. She looked like she was concentrating hard on something.

Far below, the roadster hit rocks and exploded in flame.

When Eliot's gaze returned to the sign he saw that the D was now empty. A harsh strong bitter wind was blowing. It brought with it a few grey flakes. They blew in spirals, whirling up from the burning wreckage lower down the slope. There was an acrid smell, as if rubber was on fire. As the fumes mimicked a tornado, Bix played a slow version of 'Ol' Man River'.

These flakes of ash became snow, which grew thicker. Soon the hillside had turned white. The whole of Los Angeles was blanketed by the blizzard. Everything was erased, apart from the sign and its scaffolding which stood on the slope like the skeleton of some gigantic, multi-segmented cartoon creature.

Twin ringing pulses of a phone raked an empty bedroom. Eliot stirred and began to moan. His jaw felt swollen and full of pain. He lay sprawled on some primary-colored stripes. He remembered. It was that dirty yellow rat Coleman. The lily-livered no-good two-bit son of a bitch had lacked the courage to square up to him in a fair fight. So the gutless lizard had fed him tainted nicotine to soften him up.

To his moaning Eliot added some groaning.

The pulses of sound drilled into his temple. They showed no sign of stopping.

Eliot got up and went into the bedroom. He took up the black mouth. What time was it? Early. The room held a curdled creamy light.

'Yeah,' he croaked.

'Is that Eliot?'

'Yeah.' The voice seemed familiar.

'You're Finnish!'

Who was this joker? Eliot felt he knew her. Was it an ancient wife? Or was it Mary or was it Mildred?

'I may seem foreign,' he replied. 'But I can most

emphatically assure you I am English. I have never been to Finland in my life. In fact the furthest east I've been from the island of my birth is Lowestoft. A place which is well worth a visit if you enjoy eating herrings.'

'You're stinko again, I suppose,' the woman said. Her tone was harshly critical. He recognised it. The gal with the body of a goddess and the voice of a waitress.

'Jean, dearest! Thank God you rang. I finished reading your manuscript. I have two things to tell you. Let me give you the good news first. You're an original! I've never read any other novel quite like it. It left me stunned – but in a better way than Millard Coleman did. Heck, I was every bit as electrified as Topsy the elephant! Yours is simply the most astonishing story I have ever read in my entire life! That gal Judy. I suppose in some ways she's you. I guess that was intentional, huh? Your name is four letters beginning with a "J" and so is Judy's! Wow – I mean, just, *wow*. There are so many incredible layers to the story. And the treatment of time! Forget that Prousty guy with his French cake. *Today is Tonight* is swell – just swell-in-every-page swell. When it's published it's gonna be a sensation.'

'Now listen here, Eliot Blunt, will you just shaddup and let me say what I have to say. Which is – '

'In a while, crocodile. Just lemme give you the bad news first. The fact is... well, there's just no other way of putting this. I no longer have your manuscript. It's been stolen from my apartment. It's a long story and it's not a pretty one.'

'*Shaddup!* Just shaddup!'

Eliot shaddup.

'You're finished. Got that, cluck? *Finished*. As in terminated. Over. Ended. We're through, mister. I thought you were a nice guy. I thought you were different to the others. And what do I find? The moment I'm gone you're screwing Mildred Payne. Of all people! I'm disappointed in you, Eliot Blunt. You're a jerk. In fact you're a complete bastard. You make me feel dirty. You make me feel like I need a good deep bath. You make me feel I need to wash you out of my hair. I let your fragrant liquid masculine leavings linger on me and do you know what? Now it smells like dog poop! You disgust me. And now you've been with Mildred Payne you're probably gonna have to spend a whole morning learning how to spell *gonorrhoea*.'

'But she seduced me! The bitch turned up with some irresistible liquor. She had on leather boots and not a whole lot more. I was weak, I admit it. You can't be any more disgusted with me than I am with myself.'

This was pretty good dialogue, Eliot felt. He looked for a pencil. He needed to get the words down on paper before they faded. It was a helpful exchange. He now knew Mildred's surname. This might be useful.

'Mildred Payne is a Sunset whore, Eliot. She was hired by Bello. You remember who Bello is?'

Her question sounded like information-dumping to assist an inattentive reader. This was fine by Eliot. Novelists need-ed to remember that there were a lot of lazy readers out there. Folks who had their minds on other things than prose. They needed to be reminded who was who and why Zed did zink to Zoobie. That was where the Russians and Shakespeare had the edge. They gave you the list of characters at the beginning and told you who they were.

'You mean Marino Bello, the greasy wop your beloved mother involved herself with?' he replied. 'Marino Bello of the lounge lizard's moustache? Marino Bello the self-publicising parasite and blustering narcissist?'

Harlow didn't answer his questions. All she said was: 'When he knew I'd written a novel he was determined to get hold of the manuscript. He'd heard I was interested in your intellect and your critical judgement. So he set Mildred on you. And sure enough his investment delivered. Thanks to your disgusting lack of morals, Bello now has my novel!'

'Goodness,' Eliot said. He felt someone had socked him in the solar plexus. 'But is that a bad thing? Surely he'll publish it?'

'He won't. The studio wants me as an actress, not as a writer. Bello was working for Mayer. Soon as they heard I had a narrative itch they moved to scrub it out. But I wouldn't let them. I went ahead and wrote my book. I didn't even keep a carbon copy. I gave it to the one man in the world I thought I could trust. A man who had a taste for the finest writing in the modern world. A man of integrity. A man who called himself Eliot Blunt. And what did I discover? He's just another lousy grifting hustler, same as all the others. Well, goodbye Mr Worldly Wiseman! It's over.'

The phone crackled and died.

Eliot felt the moment required a gesture on his part. 'Don't go!' he sobbed at the dead machine. Next he beat at his head with his fist, signifying distress. Next he stripped off his clothes and climbed into bed.

He slept like a baby – the trapped wind causing him to cry out, red-faced. He shrieked at the room for a while, until the witch in the apartment above banged on her floor with a broom-handle. Then, the sulphurous gas satisfyingly expelled from his body and adding to the perfume of bed sheets containing the crackling tang of Jean Harlow's dried sweat, Eliot slipped away into the Luna Park of his unconscious mind. He crossed the Bridge of Laughs, took a spin on The

Teaser and walked down a path covered in boiled eggs, crushing scores of them. He paused to pick up an unbroken one. He cracked it against his knuckle and peeled off the shell. He pressed the white glossy egg between his lips and gently ate it, a little at a time.

Inside the Tunnel of Love he found himself in a strange passageway that ended in a blue door. When he pushed it open Eliot found himself watching a man he didn't know, who was going from room to room in a big, shadowy house which had several floors and many rooms. The man's only activity was to go from room to room, glancing inside, and then shutting the door. In one room there was small naked woman who was curled up in a foetal position, sobbing quietly to herself. In another room there was the body of a man who was lying face down on the floor, his back soaked in blood. A pistol and a fedora lay nearby. The other rooms were empty.

The man grinned at Eliot and gave him a thumbs-up sign. 'You come with me, buddy,' he said. They went for a ride down Hollywood Boulevard and across Highland, west for another block, then turned right, then left again onto Franklyn Avenue. The man parked. He produced a pistol. 'Let's walk,' he said. They went a few blocks and came out on Ivar. 'In there,' he said. He was gesturing at a white building framed by lush greenery. A sign said *Hollywood Public Library*. Eliot went up four steps to the entrance porch.

Inside, the man put his phallic power device away. 'Books,' he said, his eyes full of wonder. 'Is there a greater object in the world than a book? A small portable pack of knowledge and entertainment that requires no electricity or batteries. You can't damage it too badly if you spill your beer over it. And it last for hundreds of years. Books are time-machines.

And now I must go.'

To Eliot's surprise the man shrank in size until he was no more than two or three inches high. On the lowest of the shelves a copy of *The Glass Key* lay on its side. The man lifted up the front dust-jacket and lay down inside, lowering the book's rather lurid cover upon himself until he had entirely disappeared from sight. Eliot found himself staring at a curving over-large green font which framed the frightened monochrome face of a woman with thick lips and eyes swollen with fear.

Eliot fled from the building into dazzling Californian sunlight. He shut his eyes against the glare. When he reopened them seconds later he was lying in bed. It was just after 2pm. He showered, shaved, dressed and listened to some old Bessie Smith songs. In the evening he drank enough to numb the pain of his aching jaw and the fury of Jean Harlow. He sat up late reading *A Room of One's Own*, then went to bed.

# 14

THAT NIGHT HE DREAMED he went to Manderley again. But the store had closed down. It was as derelict and empty as a critically acclaimed prize-winning realist novel. A few poignant lengths of brittle, broken spaghetti lay just inside the dusty windows. There was a poodle by the front door, emptying its bladder with the look of detached concentration found only on the faces of severely constipated university professors and sober, dieting detectives. Eliot drove to Pinkie's but got lost on the way. The *Bar-B-Que* sign didn't help none. In the end he headed for Wilshire Boulevard and went into Bullock's. Twenty minutes later he emerged with a lemon squeezer, a potato peeler, a toy elephant which hooted, two pumpkins, a couple of grapefruit and a pink banana. He paused at the east entrance to the parking lot for the pleasure of looking up at the violet light at the top of the tower. An old, white-haired crazy-looking woman in lounge pyjamas drifted over and snatched at his arm. She started to tell him the story of Miss Zella. This story was a love story, she explained, and like all love stories it took place in the past. Bitter things dried behind Miss Zella's eyes like garlic on a string before an open fire. The acrid fumes of sweet memories had reddened their rims until they shone like the used places in copper saucepans. Eliot freed himself from this garrulous Ancient Mariner's grasp and ran to his car. He halted outside a gown shop on Santa Monica Boulevard. The bright window displayed gowns cut low, back and front. Velvet trimmed with marabou, silver lamé, silk, fur... He felt he'd look good in any of them. Maybe he had transvestite inclinations which he'd suppressed. Perhaps Harlow would come back to him if he dressed like she did. But he felt he'd like to continue with male underwear.

Next he went to the Chinese Theater. A fellow from central casting wearing a coolie's hat was standing outside it holding a sheet of paper. Eliot stepped out of the car and went over to him.

'Glad you could make it, buddy,' the ersatz Chinaman said. 'And on time too!' The actor cleared his throat, focused his gaze on the sheet of paper, and began to recite.

In the season when blossoms fall from cherry trees,
On a day when hummingbirds flew from bough to bough,
You said you must stay, because your Buick had a flat;
I said I must go, because my agent was waiting.

'That's beautiful,' Eliot said. Tears poured down his face. Soon Hollywood Boulevard was flooded. He swam to a Mexican fan palm and began climbing up it. Below him he noticed the old woman from the parking lot. She was squatting and holding a copy of *The Los Angeles Times*. 'You come down here right now young man!' she shouted. 'You're wiping away my dream.'

Eliot turned away and continued his ascent. He was almost at the top, where the views were spectacular, when he slipped. The floodwater cushioned his fall. The salty liquid swept him off to a little restaurant where he dried out, alone at a table under a canopy of horse-chestnuts. The dazzling sun had turned his last few asparagus stalks to a chromatic xylophone. Then some large black object in the sky slid by, screening the ball of hydrogen and helium above Eliot's eaterie. He sucked in cold air infused with sea fog.

Next thing it was Monday morning. Eliot drove to the M-G-M lot. He moved through the small crowd of fans clustered by the arch. There was the usual spasm of disappointment as they saw he was nobody.

He parked. As Eliot approached the writers' building he saw her – striding along, tall and slim and radiant. She was just what he needed, now Harlow had dumped him.

'Mary!'

She saw him, looked scared, and began to run. Just moments later she disappeared behind the wooden horse of Troy. Eliot went in pursuit.

A line of Roman centurions came past, chewing gum and smoking. He pushed his way through them. Mary, two hundred yards away, was emerging from behind a beached paddle-steamer. She ran on, passing a Dutch windmill and vanished from sight behind the Swiss alps.

Eliot caught up with her in the Far East, hiding behind a Buddha.

'Mary, darling!'

But she pushed him away. Her eyes flashed. 'Stay away from me!'

'But dearest – '

'I'm not your dearest. Don't call me that. Just stay away from me. Don't you see, Millard knows all about us! He's having me followed by a private dick.'

'A private dick!' Eliot looked nervously round, to see if the Austrian was lurking with his notebook.

'I need you to go – *now*.'

'Did you know your husband came to see me? He gave me a doped cigarette. Then when I couldn't defend myself he punched me on the jaw, the cowardly rat.'

Her eyes widened. 'That's terrible!'

It was. This kind of material wasn't particularly original. 'But does originality matter? People like familiarity, don't you think? They want clichés – especially romantic ones. The cheating wife is always good for a plot line. As is the angry cuckolded husband.'

'Just stop talking and go. *Please.*'

'Human kind cannot bear very much reality.'

'*Shaddup!*'

Eliot reached out to calm her but she threw him off. 'Listen, big boy. I have a very thick pack of dreams. The game ain't over yet. But sorry, mister – you're in the discard pile. Now be a pal and beat it.'

She'd loosened up a little and when Eliot lurched forwards and smashed his lips against hers he took her by surprise. She couldn't say anything because he kept the pressure up. Then he put his arms around her and crushed her against him.

'Oh God,' she sobbed, pulling back. Next her scarlet-tipped fingers were dragging her skirt up. She wasn't wearing knickers. Her back pressed itself against the Buddha's left ear. Her nails dug into Eliot. The pain excited him. He felt blood trickling like lukewarm water down the backs of his thighs. The Buddha rocked a little but didn't topple. It continued smiling blandly as the cliché came to fruition.

Afterwards she brushed flakes of gold paint from her bottom. 'You go first.'

'Okay.'

'We can never do this again.'

'If you say so.'

'I do say so. This Gautama is no more than lath and plaster and painted board and it's rotten – as rotten as my heart.'

'Okay.'

The Buddha continued to project a smug self-satisfaction as Eliot made his way back across Europe. He didn't look back to see if Mary was following.

*

Eliot hadn't been to his office since the quake. Entering it he found it undamaged apart from one broken item.

William Shakespeare had been shaken from his perch and lay on the floor, shattered. Both legs were snapped off at the knee and the head was missing. Eliot was shocked to see that Shakespeare was hollow. He'd always somehow assumed he was solid all the way through.

He had to get down on his hands and knees to locate the head. It was wedged behind the filing cabinet. Shakespeare stared at him like an egg with eyes and a philosophy degree. Eliot used the hand end of a fly swat to manoeuvre the bard out. He had an uneasy feeling that Dr Freud was watching him and writing something in his notebook.

When he examined the statuette's jagged parts it was obvious that the playwright was in a condition every bit as bad as Humpty Dumpty's. Too bad. Eliot clutched Shakespeare's head in his fist. It felt smooth and peculiarly warm. Something pale and sticky had trickled from a tiny hole at the top of the cranium. The spectral Austrian's stiff plump pen went haywire.

The shins and the rest followed the same trajectory as the bard's cream-colored brainbox. The fragments clattered as they met the bin's tinny stained interior.

Having tidied up the mess Eliot felt he was due a liquid reward. He settled for liquor and brought out a bottle from the bottom drawer of the steel cabinet. The hootch illuminated his guts. From the top drawer he took out his *Orlando* treatment. It was almost complete. All he needed to sketch was the final shoot-out and it would be done. Or at least, first-draft-done. Hell, Eliot was an experienced operator. He knew that a treatment and a script went through multiple versions before the shooting one.

He read what he'd written so far while he was finishing his second modest tumbler. He was just pouring himself a third glass – well, it was almost 11am and that seemed like a responsible time for anyone to start refreshing themselves for the day ahead – when someone rapped on his door.

He guessed it was Mary. She'd dodged the gumshoe and was here for second helpings. That was swell by him. Eliot had always been a second-helpings kind of guy. You name it: liquor, plum pudding, chocolate ice-cream... Heck, he was still only thirty-two. His chamber was full again. He was in his prime, full of vigour. He had the ammo. Come and get it, candy-girl!

But it was not Mary. It was an affable, fatherly guy wearing a cardigan and a tie. The spectacles added to his harmless ordinary-guy-approaching-middle-age appearance. The sort who wouldn't hurt a fly. He might have been a college professor who wrote verse and fancied himself as the Keats of Westwood. But underneath that genial exterior was a man of steel with a heart of ice and in the right pocket of that big, floppy, too-long tweed jacket was something that weighed a lot heavier than his conscience.

It was Whitey Hendry, chief of the studio's police force. An ex-cop with top connections in the LAPD. He was Mr Security, incorporating garbage disposal, sanitation and cleaning. The kind of guy who was *liked and respected by all*. Especially the stars. He knew all the dirt. He flushed it away. Afterwards there was only the aroma of roses. He made damned sure the cheeks the studio displayed to the world were flawless vanilla.

His smile was like that of the M-G-M lion's. He gave Eliot that ol' leonine grin as he stepped into the shining sunlit room. His drooping arm stiffened and raised itself. He extended a hand.

Friendly handshake!

'How's it going, Eliot?'

'Pretty good, Mr Hendry.'

'That's good to hear, son.'

A cloud of dust moved slowly in a beam of golden sunlight. Dust, Eliot thought, is something we don't think about enough. It's always there, in every room. Where does it come from? It moves in the air. People swallow it, breathe it, try to cough it out. It drops and gathers like ash. But no matter how much you sweep it away, it always comes back. In fact it never leaves you. It's there when you enter a building and it's there when you leave. You can never get rid of it. It's like a love you once enjoyed but now it's gone yet you can never shake it off. It does bad things to you. It becomes an irritant.

All over the lot you saw and heard people coughing. At every table in the commissary there was usually someone hunched over, pressing a palm or a fist or a handkerchief to an open mouth.

The title of a possible novel broke through the crust of Eliot's thoughts. *Question The Dust*. Wow! A classic! But Hendry's dialogue dragged him away from his brown study and handcuffed him to his office chair.

The ex-cop's eyes glinted like glass on the bridge of a destroyer at dawn. 'The fact is, Eliot, Millard Coleman doesn't want you on the lot. I'm sure you don't need me to spell out why that should be. It strikes me that a guy like you knows a lot more spelling than a lot of the folks round here. Folks who'd look as blank and speechless as the crown of a homburg if you mentioned uxorodespotism or velleity. And don't ask them to spell yacht!'

Eliot did not reply.

'Also, you're an alcoholic.'

Eliot did not wish to address the first topic of discussion but he felt indignant regarding the second. He gestured dramatically. 'Hell, so are all the other writers! So are half the actors! So are the directors, the executives. Frankly I wouldn't be surprised if the goddam M-G-M lion likes a drop of whiskey with his meat.'

Whitey Hendry chuckled. 'Very droll, Mr Blunt. For your information I'm a teetotaller. As all decent God-fearing American citizens should be. But leaving such matters aside, the fact is I'm here to tell you that your studio pass has been cancelled and your services as a writer are no longer required.'

'You can't do this to me!'

'Oh, but I can,' Hendry said.

The dialogue was tired. It needed something to liven it up. Another gulp or two of tonic. Gulp-gulp. The hootch gave Eliot courage. He felt more than ever like a Dashiell Hammett hero. 'Let's just say I don't feel like leaving. I have work to do. Important work.'

Hendry coughed. The dust had gotten to him too. Then he shouted: '*Boys!*'

The door was thrown open by a tough-looking man with a fiery face and a broken nose. Behind him loomed a scowling seven-foot giant with a stomach like that of a whale. He had a seven-inch scar down the left side of his face. His temperament appeared taciturn.

'Boys, I'd like you to meet Mr Blunt. Mr Blunt, I'd like you to meet Jack Flack and Herb Wharton. These boys will be escorting you off the premises once we've concluded our little conversation.' Hendry gave his thugs a wave. 'Thanks boys.'

Broken Nose nodded. The door closed.

'Let me level with you, Eliot. Millard Coleman draws some water in these parts but maybe not enough to get rid of a top talent just because the TT is banging his wife. And let's face it, buddy, Coleman ain't exactly a saint when it comes to country matters. As for the boozing... Hell, yes. This whole damn cinematic operation floats on a lake that's eight parts whiskey to two of water. But there's something else. Something that counts for a whole heap more than what's just been spilled. And that something is this.'

He paused, dramatically. The guy had seen too many movies, Eliot felt.

The seconds ticked by, marked by a vocal grandfather clock which surely hadn't been there in the earlier scenes.

Hendry produced a pipe from the other pocket to the one where he kept his gun. Maybe it was ballast.

'This is not a pipe,' he said, winking, as he laid the pipe on the desk and rummaged for tobacco. Eliot said nothing. He'd heard the joke before. Next Hendry made a big thing of lighting his pipe. His thick fingers poked, fiddled and pressed as they applied themselves to the draught hole and the chamber.

At last the ex-cop managed to set fire to the crushed tobacco. A toxic stench filled the room as the smoke expanded, masking the tongues of dust. Hendry sucked contentedly on the stem, exhaling fumes like a dragon. At long last (another good title, Eliot thought) he arrived, grunting, at his narrative climax.

'The big thing – the really big thing – is that Miss Harlow doesn't want you around. She says if she sees you on the lot it will only upset her. And Miss Harlow is a major property, as

I'm sure you appreciate. What Miss Harlow wants, Miss Harlow gets. So to put it bluntly, Blunt, we don't want your miserable lowly presence disturbing a major star and a director who's going places. Got that, buddy?'

'Hold your horses, cowboy. I work for Irving Thalberg. I'm on a special commission. I work exclusively for him.'

Hendry's crinkly eyes developed some extra crinkles. He gazed bleakly back. 'Mr Thalberg has spoken to me. He wants you to know you no longer work for him. He doesn't need you any more. Those treatments you gave him – something to do with a wolf, right? – well they've been canned. Apparently the crazy dame who wrote the novels won't sell the film rights. The dumb bitch won't even come to Hollywood. I shipped one of my boys over the ocean to check her out. He said she was screwy. She hangs out with pansies in a sick little town called Bloomsburg. He came back a little screwy himself. He was driven mad by sea-sickness. He told me he'd been where the heel-headed dogfish barks its nose on Ahab's void and forehead and the sea-gulls blink their heavy lids. The poor sap had to be sent to an institution. That's what hanging out with writers can do to even the toughest feller.'

'The poor, poor chap.' Eliot managed a wry smile, slightly toasted. 'As a profession we're dangerous to know, I'll grant you that. We're sick, mad, drunk, cruel, lecherous, treacherous, jealous, envious, greedy, shallow, ambitious, devious, unprincipled, depraved, unreliable and wholly narcissistic. Our egos might well have been designed by Ferdinand von Zeppelin. Bloated and delicate and full of gas and wind, signifying nothing. And easily blown off-course.'

Hendry expelled more noxious smoke. 'So let's cut to the chase, wise-ass. Apart from your little fling with the widow, there's the matter of her novel. From a company point of view both are dynamite which could blow our humble vessel out of the water. That's why I'm firing you with rewards.'

Hendry reached into his wallet and handed Eliot a cheque.

'Two thousand bucks a month, for the foreseeable future. You stay away from the studio. You keep your monkey-mouth zipped. Do that and Mr Thalberg will have you back. Maybe not next month or the month after that. Maybe not even until the fall of thirty-three. But keep your nose clean and play your aces, son, and you'll be back. In the meantime you go write your great American novel or whatever in hell your type does with all that free time. But just remember. If there's a whisper of scandal about Miss Harlow, or a word about her secret novel, the cheques stop. And more than that. You'll be getting a late-night visit from Jack and Herb. You wouldn't want that. After a social call from them you'll be spending a lot of time at the fracture clinic and with your dentist.' Hendry stood up, scowling. 'Is that understood?'

Eliot nodded. 'I understand, sir.'

Now the chief was smiling again. Big, friendly smiles like a waiter hustling for a tip. 'That's good. That's very good. That's exceptionally good. It's always a pleasure to meet a fellow who shows some solid common sense. I've always liked limeys. They got their heads screwed on right. And they're mighty good at kneeling.' He winked.

At the door he paused. It was another trick he'd learned from the movies. 'A word to the wise. It might be a good idea to leave town for a while. Word has reached my hairy old ears that Millard Coleman has set up a meeting with a hit-man. I have a notion who the target might be.'

'Goodness,' Eliot whispered. His face had turned the color of oatmeal.

'Go visit Yurp.'

'Eh?'

'Yurp. You know, Paree, France. The famous palace of King Buckingham. The colossus in Rome, the pyramids. Shit like that. Go back to where you came from. I took a look at your personnel file before I came to see you. I'm sure Cocksworld must be a mighty fine place. Go visit your mother.'

'My mother's dead.'

'Well, buddy, if you stay in L.A. you might be joining her real soon.'

Scar-face and broken-nose led him in silence to his car and watched him depart the lot. Eliot drove first to Korzienowski's. He'd had a message to say the bookseller had new stock in which might interest a connoisseur like himself.

When he got there he found it was his precious Woolfs. Treacherous, lying Mildred Payne had sold them all. Eliot was reunited with his beloved autographed copy of *The Waves*.

'As you good customer, Mr Bent, I give you this for bonus. You speak German, no?'

'*Ja.*'

The old Pole chuckled, exposing a mouth which was putting on an exhibition of dreary avant-garde art involving yellow pegs and rabbit-holes.

'Is very strange book. And much filth. You like, I think.'

Eliot wondered why the bookseller sounded like a Mexican. But it was best not to think about what other people did in private. He took the slim book and glanced at the title. *Traumnovelle*. He'd never heard of either the book or the novelist. That meant it was probably a cult classic in the making.

'*Muchas gracias amigo.*'

'*To nic.*'

# 15

IN LONDON THERE WAS a store on Charing Cross Road which sold five-days-old copies of *The Los Angeles Times* at four times the price he'd paid in Echo Park. Eliot went there every morning and then on to a coffee bar on Chandos Place to read some of it before The Lamb and Flag opened.

It was on the morning of his twentieth day in the capital that a fist in an iron glove hit him hard in the guts. It was there on the front page – stark, brutal, horrible.

SILENT STAR MARY LYONS SLAIN.

Eliot's body convulsed. The coffee cup tipped on its white saucer. A surge of brown fluid saturated the lower half of the newspaper and dripped from the table's edge, on to his trousers. He felt the coffee's sting. He swore and jerked his wooden chair back.

The waitress and the establishment's three other customers gazed at Eliot curiously. Eventually the waitress came over with a cloth and mopped the table.

'Would you like another coffee, sir?'

Eliot shook his head.

His body was trembling. The newspaper shook when he tried to pick it up. A sodden section came away like a rotten tooth. The simile seemed a little on the tired side and when he went to sleep that night in his rented room on the street where Benjamin Franklin and Herman Melville had once lived, Eliot found himself listening to a dentist with a Bronx accent who explained that teeth like this should be pulverized and then mixed with grated chocolate, making an excellent fertiliser for carrots.

Leaving the dentistry, Eliot hurried to London Bridge station, where he caught a train to Canterbury. It began to spit with rain on the journey. By the time the train reached its destination it was pouring down. Mary was waiting for him on the platform as the train pulled in. She was wearing a white raincoat and holding a man's black umbrella. Eliot opened the heavy metal door and jumped from the carriage. A smear of oil covered his hand. They embraced. 'A sad tale's best for winter,' she said, in that faint whispery unforgettable voice of hers. And then she dissolved and he was left staring at a broken umbrella. The wind pushed it around, half-inflating it. The brolly resembled a large bird with a broken wing, repeatedly attempting to fly. But that bird would never fly again. When night fell the rats would get it.

The story was a simple one. Mary had been walking to her car which was parked in back of a store on Central Avenue. She was carrying shopping and was opening her car door when some punk tried to rob her. She fought back and the punk shot her four times. He took her purse and ran off into the twilight. The cops had a description – a white man, in his twenties, scruffy-looking. Mary was dead by the time the ambulance arrived. The purse and the killer had not yet been found.

Hollywood mourned one of its legends. A week later there was the funeral. Lots of flowers, a variety of celebrities. The widower wore a black suit and a look of grief which was tainted by a faint smirk.

*You lousy lug*, Eliot thought. *You couldn't snuff me, so you had her snuffed instead.*

But sometimes life is like a novel written by Charles Dickens, full of remarkable coincidences and with a delightful and heart-warming conclusion. Exactly forty days after Mary's murder Millard Coleman was on the flight from Kansas City that slid into the top of a flat-topped mountain when the plane was just twelve minutes from landing at Glendale Airport. Everyone on board escaped apart from Millard. He was still tangled up in his belt, feverishly trying to unbuckle it, when the fuselage lit up with a spreading flood of fire. The survivors gathered at a safe distance, listening to the director's terrible screams. And then the fire grew more intense and that stretched, howling voice fell abruptly silent. Something exploded and blew its fierce breath over what by now were the witnesses to a cremation.

Eliot felt a huge relief. It was now safe for him to return to L.A. and resume his life as a writer in the city of broken dreamers. As that year came to an end Eliot spent the loneliest Christmas of his life in a room in a run-down carpenter's gothic house off Washington Boulevard. He got by on cold beans with Scotch eggs and plenty of hootch. He didn't have to live like that – the M-G-M cheques kept coming – but the ambiance suited him. It felt like the start of something but he only found out later what it was.

It was his lost decade. He became just another poor sap who'd gone to grease in Hollywood. He drank heavily and worked on *Of Flesh and Age* but the manuscript never really came to life. He achieved 500 pages of typescript and then gave up and started a new book, *She Never Said Goodbye*. It was about a talented writer who is destroyed by his affair with a famous movie actress. He finished that one – it came out at 247 pages – but he couldn't find an agent who was even half-interested. He tried all the publishing houses, from the big ones to the littlest and all he ever got was silence or the bum's rush.

He went to a nearby movie theatre to see *Dinner at Eight* and *Bombshell* and came out in tears. He started a relationship with a ginger-haired cutie who said her name was Eileen Fromsett. She lived in Long Beach. It was the second Friday in March and they had the whole weekend to spend together. He was at her place and they were in the first throes of their passion. They accomplished for the first and last time what would many decades later join the inventory of Hollywood clichés, i.e. simultaneous orgasm. It was 5.54pm, Pacific Standard Time. The power of their ecstasy toppled her treasured vase from Cuernavaca, which crashed to the floor and broke into nineteen pieces. The bedroom window shattered and the little pile of books on her bedside table flew out into the street. It was goodbye to her editions of *Jungle Girl*, *The Clue in the Diary*, *The Tenth Moon*, *Keeper of the Keys*, *The Purple Prince of Oz* and *While the Clock Ticked*. Shocked by all this turbulence the lovers separated, wiped themselves and stood naked at the empty window frame, gazing out. 'Quake,' Eileen said.

Just up the street fallen masonry had crushed three people. Their legs protruded from the rubble in a symmetrical oval pattern, as if a giant spider had been squashed. Eileen and Eliot began coughing. The air was murky with drifts of dark reddish dust. They did not see the photographer in the building opposite. 'Naked couple at the window after the Long Beach earthquake' was not published until 1972 and is now widely regarded as one of the classic photographs of historic California.

The cheques from M-G-M kept coming. Eliot enquired about returning to work on the lot but a velvet voice informed him there were no openings. He cracked a savage male joke about passes and access and she put the phone down. Eliot broke up with Eileen the following year. She said he was an impossible character. It was impossible to go on loving someone who didn't believe in teknonymy. They'd quarrelled with increasing frequency. He deplored her telamnesia and her taste in fiction. What grated most of all was her habit of grinding her teeth when she was asleep. He strongly suspected that in her dreams she was a tiger and he was a gazelle. His own dreaming was like that of a novelist who writes a successful novel and then just goes on repeating it, the story becoming more and more tired with each re-telling. His uneventful nocturnal plot always involved the man who was going from room to room in a big, shadowy house which had several floors and many rooms. The man's only activity was to go from room to room, glancing inside, and then shutting the door. Sometimes the man was Louis B. Mayer, sometimes he was Irving Thalberg and sometimes he was Whitey Hendry. But most of the time he was a stranger.

That was the year he went to see *The Girl from Missouri*. It was a mistake. It churned his guts to see Harlow up there, her form massively enlarged. Her voice boomed and crackled across the auditorium. She was Glumdalclitch and he was Gulliver. His mood was low until Korzienowski left a message. He had something for him. It was a book about a notorious pornographer. 'I sink your kind of book,' the old Pole croaked, with a frog chuckle. It was – very much so. Eliot was enthralled by this book about the infamous 'thin man' of a notoriously dirty book. The story began high up on the Zürichberg, beyond the Fluntern tram terminus. Night was falling. Wasps pestered the outdoor drinkers. A tall slender man came into the garden from the restaurant. He was a dark mass against the orange light of the restaurant glass door but he carried his head with the chin uptilted so that his face collected cool light from the sky. His walk suggested that of a wading heron. From his heavily glassed eyes it was plain that the transition from light interior to the twilight zone of the garden had made him unsure of a space cluttered with iron chairs, tables and many other obstructive nouns.

Another year began. There were a lot of lost weekends in '35. Eliot was half-stewed when he watched *Reckless* and three-quarters stewed at *China Seas*. He slept through most of that last movie. He had a spell of walking around Beverly Hills drunk, screaming 'Where does Glumdalclitch live?' The cops were called but he outwitted them by falling asleep behind hedges and amid beds of thriving geraniums. Once he fell into a pond and stayed underwater until dawn, breathing by mouth through a hollow stalk. He only sobered up when Korzienowski sent word of a new import. A book written, surprisingly, by a woman. Unless 'Enid Welsford' was the pen name of a lusty male with a twinkle in his eye. 'Kunz,' Korzienowki whispered, grinning and pointing with a nicotine-stained forefinger. The tattoo of an anchor was exposed on his wrinkled wrist. Eliot nodded coolly and took the book home.

It did not disappoint. The book's range was wide. It described the adventures of Kunz at the court of the Emperor Maximilian I. Water was involved – and on one occasion, a rope and some swans. Kunz led to Fugger, Arcemalle to Crapelet and Coq and *The Devil is an Ass*. There was Delia the dwarf. There was a Hooker. There was an account of the queer symptom of a madman. It was dark, weird stuff. But at the end there was a rant about Hollywoodland. Enid Welsford didn't much like movies, that was clear. She deplored the *mechanistic and impersonal aspect of the cinematograph*. It had killed off something special. Nobody cared about actors any more. *Legend has been slow to gather round film-stars*. People simply weren't interested in the lives of actors and actresses. In her serene certainties she reminded Eliot of his old friend, the polar bear.

On Christmas Eve he went to see *Riffraff*. It made him sick to see that one of his old ideas had been adapted, without a credit. As for the scene where Harlow, having hurled the fish, falls backwards and opens her legs wide, that sent a stab of desire through his aching, restless groin. Before he knew it there were fireworks spurting and crackling across the city's twinkling plain, jets of pleasure, sweet silvery ecstasies, little dying shivers of gold and silver. It was New Year's Eve and everyone was happy, everyone was carousing with friends and lovers. Everyone except Eliot Blunt. He sat alone in his cold room in a rotting house, eating a Scotch egg and drinking bourbon. He wondered what 1936 would bring.

What it brought was February and *Wife Vs. Secretary*. There was a new maturity about Harlow's acting, now. In June came *Suzy*, in October *Libeled Lady*. His miserable life was punctuated by these regular reminders of everything he'd lost.

That fall, out of the blue, into the black, Thalberg had died. Another obstacle to Eliot's return to M-G-M had gone. But there was one left, which seemed irremovable. Harlow was working her ass off, turning out film after film. And Eliot knew that as long as she was around he could never return to M-G-M. Word had reached him that he was still regarded as an embarrassment. They kept him on the payroll. The world must not know about her foolish awful degrading humiliating momentary affair with a nonentity. And her secret novel must remain secret.

This was the year Eliot wrote a short, intense, troubled work about Eddie Hammer, a brilliant Hollywood screen-writer destroyed by his alcoholism and his brief affair with a screen goddess – a fictional star called June Hollow. The manuscript was rejected by all the big boys but was finally accepted by Zealous Press, a small outfit on the edge of Watts. Their only demand was that Eliot adopt a more suitable name. 'Blunt', they felt, was somehow off-putting. He suggested 'Eric Blare' or 'Norbert Vronsky'. In the end it was agreed that the book should go out as the work of 'Ephraim Bullitt'.

*Dissecting a Heart* received a rave review in *Mojave Desert* magazine, which called it 'scorching and arid' and commented, 'reading it would sure make anyone build up a thirst'. *Santa Monica on Sunday* found it 'unreadable in the best sense'. One week after publication the publishers went bust and almost all copies were sent to the dump, the dump, the dump. Only twelve copies of the novel are known to survive, commanding as much as seven dollars fifty from dealers in second-hand books.

Eliot never seemed able to match the success of that work. He examined his two old unpublished novels, decided they were second-rate, and destroyed them. He started writing a sequel to his Ephraim Bullit book – *Falling Downstairs, Naked* – but it stalled half way through. Matters weren't helped by *Personal Property*'s release in March. And then, in that first terrible week in June, there was a small news item. Jean Harlow was unwell. But it was nothing serious. She was resting at home. On June 3 her physician, Dr E. C. Fishbaugh, told an Associated Press reporter that there was nothing to worry about. Miss Harlow had a cold. She was resting comfortably and feeling much better. But on the evening of Sunday 6 June 1937 she was taken by ambulance to the Good Samaritan Hospital downtown. The banal smooth incompetent smug Fishbaugh of the polar bear fraternity was a bow-tied dolt who'd failed to recognise the classic symptoms of kidney disease. His patient slipped into a coma and was placed in an oxygen tent. At 11.37am on Monday Jean Harlow's heart stopped. The following month Eliot was in the long queue to see her final movie, *Saratoga*. He was not the only member of the audience to weep.

After that the cheques stopped and Eliot went back to working for M-G-M. They loaned him out to Columbia to do some last-minute rewrites on *Lost Horizon*. This was maybe what led to him becoming part of the Hollywood Raj and hanging out with James Hilton and Ronald Colman. But he also forged a friendship with a washed-up writer called Scottie. The poor sap had it worse than Eliot. He'd been big in the Flapper Age but fashions had changed and now nobody read him anymore. Scottie and Eliot drank highballs together at the Garden of Allah, talking about whatever writers talk about. Money mostly, and broads. Later, after Scottie dropped dead, the obituaries were cruel. The *Chicago Daily News* really rubbed it in. The paper said – *pow!* – Scottie was almost as remote from contemporary interest as – *wham!* – the authors of the blue-chip stock certificates of 1929. No one was mistaking a story writer for the Herald of an Era. But it was true – his readership had gone. His last royalty statement earned him an unlucky thirteen dollars and thirteen cents. *Tender is the Night* had sold nine copies and *The Great Gatsby* seven.

By now there was war in Yurp. Eliot didn't qualify to take up arms for either the land of his birth or, later, of his adoption. He was in bad shape, physically. His hands shook and a colony of wild bees had made their home inside his head. The only way to flush them out was with liquor. He did some rewrites on *Random Harvest* and – loaned out again, this time to Paramount – on *The Lost Weekend*. But there were still no screen credits.

During these years Eliot wondered why Harlow's novel still hadn't been published. After the success of *Saratoga* the studio could have made a mint out of *Today is Tonight*. It was incomprehensible why the manuscript stayed locked up in somebody's safe. He began to think it must have been destroyed. Or were the Illuminati somehow involved?

He also wondered about Mildred Payne. One day he'd be walking along Sunset and she'd be coming the other way. Then she'd see him and hurry towards him and they'd embrace. She'd be older, now, looking tired. She'd smile; she'd be so happy to see him again. Eliot didn't hold grudges; he'd kiss her back, with more passion than was appropriate to the situation. Then they'd go off to a hotel and climb into bed. Afterwards they'd talk about the years and what had happened in their lives.

But that never happened. He never saw Mildred again.

After the war there are suggestions that Eliot may have worked with Hitchcock, although no documentary evidence survives. It's known that he married a wealthy widow called Alice Land. They lived in her big house in the Hollywood Hills. Eliot suffered from heart trouble and took forty-eight drops of Digitalin every night. But the marriage didn't last. Alice described him as controlling and prone to mood swings. Plus, she said, Eliot drank too much. He seemed broken and lost.

Back then everything was changing. A few years after the war ended, if you walked through the residential sections of Beverly Hills, you'd see a flickering blue light in the windows of the houses that you passed. Instead of going to see a movie everyone was staying home to watch *I Love Lucy* on a walnut-panelled four-legged box with a magic screen. What an invention! No more having to organise a babysitter. No more having to get the car out of the garage. No more having to drive through the night and park and then walk an arduous half a block to the movie theatre. When it rained you got wet. But at home you were dry and warm. You need no longer suffer that gnawing, drawn-out fear that at the very last moment, just as the lights dimmed, a fat slob stinking of popcorn and with too much hair or a large hat would disturb the row in front in order to lower monstrous buttocks on to the seat exactly aligned with your own.

Alice herself preferred staying in to watch TV to going to the movies. Movies didn't interest her. That was part of the problem. Eliot was always having weird dreams about film stars and people, Alice complained. He bored her crazy, going on about them. He was always returning to the same places and meeting the same people, over and over again. But everyone Eliot met, if they spoke at all, said they were lost for words.

One dream he kept having involved this ship anchored at a quayside in a thick sea fog. It kept blowing its foghorn. Eliot went on board and down several flights of iron stairs. He came to a long corridor and at the end of it was a woman clothed only in transparent scarves. She was doing a strange wild dance and laughing. Then the woman shrank in size and turned into a tiny white dot, like when you turned the TV off. But the dot didn't die out. Instead it expanded and became a wall of whiteness. It surged towards Eliot. He said he knew what it was. It was white ink! It was coming for him. It was going to erase him. And then the wave went over him and he was gone.

'I couldn't go on living with a man like that,' Alice said. 'He was too intense, too acrid. All these dreams that kept repeating themselves. It was a lot of nonsense.'

She lit a cigarette. Drifts of thin smoke filled the room, killing the sweet sickly odour of air freshener and corruption.

She raised a bony, wrinkled arm and gestured feebly at the room. It was strangely bare of furniture now. Beyond the window a mist had crawled across the neighbourhood, obliterating the lawns and the line of hibiscus bushes by the fence. It came on, a cold tide covering the distant bed of Sticky Phacelia and Silverpuffs and the white roses which had been hanging down across the pane.

Somewhere out there a dog started barking, which set off the hoarse hysterical screechings of a macaw.

Alice's voice was flaky with rust and almost inaudible. She sounded and looked like Mary Lyons might have looked if she'd lived into extreme old age. The ghost of a once-beautiful woman was incarcerated behind a grid of wrinkles as dense as the mesh on an aviary.

She sucked her cheeks in, as if she was struggling to breathe. She coughed, coughed again, then drew more smoke into her ancient sooty lungs. 'I mean... '

Alice raised her withered, dappled arm again. It was like someone playing a deathbed scene, about to make some grand statement of love or forgiveness. Her eyes were lively with amusement. Her face stretched its fissures as she cracked open a tight, narrow, geriatric smile.

'Who ever heard of white ink?'


After the marriage foundered Eliot went south, to Mexico, and there the trail goes cold. He was last heard of in Quauhnahuac, renting a room from a man called Clarence.

He told people he'd been diagnosed with alcoholic cardio-myopathy and he was there to rest and fill up a notebook with recherché phrases.

One day he caught the bus to Xochimilco and did not come back.